CHAPTERS AND CHORDS

A STORY OF MUSIC, WORDS, AND THE LOVE THAT REFUSED TO FADE

SREEJA SELVAM

Made with ❤ on the Notion Press Platform
www.notionpress.com

Contents

Contents

Author's Note

Dear Reader,

Chapters & Chords is not just a love story. It's a journey through music, words, and the spaces between them. It's about the dreams we chase, the people we meet along the way, and the choices that define us.

Aarav and Taarika's story is one of love, but also of self-discovery. Because sometimes, love isn't about losing yourself in someone else—it's about finding yourself in the spaces they leave behind.

If you've ever had a dream so big it scared you, if you've ever loved someone in a way that felt like a song waiting to be finished, then this story is for you.

Thank you for stepping into their world. I hope it touches your heart as much as it touched mine while writing it.

With love and stories,
Sreeja Selvam

Acknowledgements

Writing Chapters & Chords has been a journey of emotions, passion, and endless inspiration, and I am deeply grateful to everyone who made this book possible.

First and foremost, I thank my readers—those who believe in love stories, in the power of music and words, and in the magic of second chances. Your love for romance and storytelling is what brings stories like this to life.

To my family, who have always supported my dreams, even when they seemed impossible. Your encouragement, love, and belief in me have given me the strength to keep writing.

To my friends, who have been my biggest cheerleaders—thank you for listening to my endless story ideas, for sharing your thoughts, and for pushing me to bring this book to life.

Finally to all the writers and musicians who inspire me every day—this story is a tribute to the beauty of creativity, the emotions hidden in lyrics, and the stories waiting to be told.

This book is for everyone who has ever fallen in love between the lines of a song, a story, or a moment.

With all my heart,
Sreeja Selvam

1
The First Note of Fate

Aarav had never believed in destiny. To him, life was a series of random events strung together by chance. Some moments were fleeting, others left behind echoes, but none were preordained.

Yet, as he stepped off the train into the quiet town of Manesar, a strange feeling settled in his chest—a weightless, inexplicable anticipation, as though he was about to write the most important song of his life.

The station was nearly empty, save for a few tired commuters and chai vendors calling out their last sales of the evening. The air smelled of rain-soaked earth, rusted train tracks, and something unexpected—fresh ink. Aarav adjusted the strap of his guitar case on his shoulder, taking in the town that was meant to be his escape.

He hadn't planned to be here. Manesar wasn't on his list of places to visit. But when the chaos of Mumbai, the noise of expectations, and the pressure to make something of his music became too much, he had boarded the first train out. And now, here he was—standing at the edge of something unfamiliar, a town where he was nobody, where he could exist without the weight of his past trailing behind him.

His feet carried him through the winding streets, past dimly lit bookshops and old tea stalls. Manesar was different from Mumbai. There was a slowness here, a quiet charm in the way people lingered over their conversations instead of rushing to the next thing. He exhaled, feeling the tension in his chest ease just a little.

Then, he saw it.

A place he had read about in online "The Lantern Library".

It wasn't just any library. It was an old heritage building, its wooden doors framed with ivy and its windows glowing with the golden warmth of old stories. Inside, towering bookshelves lined the walls, vintage lamps cast soft pools of light, and cozy corners invited readers to lose themselves in words. A place where silence spoke louder than noise.

It felt like a refuge. And after months of feeling lost, a refuge was exactly what Aarav needed.

As he pushed open the heavy door, the scent of aged paper and coffee filled his senses. The wooden floors creaked under his boots as he wandered past shelves stacked with classics, poetry, and music theory books. His fingers grazed the spine of a familiar title when movement near the stained-glass window caught his eye.

A girl.

She sat alone at a dimly lit table, completely lost in the pages of a tattered notebook. Her long, wavy hair cascaded over her shoulders, partially obscuring her face. A pen rested between her fingers, tapping absently against the table as if her thoughts were moving faster than she could write. There was a small crease between her brows, a frown of concentration, and the kind that came from pouring your soul onto paper.

Aarav found himself staring.

"She's here every evening," an old librarian muttered as she passed by, catching his gaze. "Writes like the words might disappear if she doesn't."

A writer.

Aarav smirked, a flicker of curiosity sparking within him.

He didn't believe in love at first sight. He barely believed in love at all.

But something about her made his fingers itch to pick up his guitar. Something about her felt like a melody waiting to be played.

Just then, as if sensing his presence, she looked up.

For a fleeting second, their eyes met - his deep brown ones searching, hers unreadable, guarded yet holding a quiet intensity.

The moment stretched.

Then, just as quickly, she blinked and returned to her notebook, as if he didn't exist.

Aarav let out a breath he hadn't realized he was holding.

Interesting.

Little did he know, this was just the first note in the song of their fate.

2
Lyrics in the Silence

Taarika had always loved the hush of The Lantern Library—the way stories breathed between old pages, the way silence wasn't empty but full of untold tales.

For as long as she could remember, writing had been more than a passion. It was her escape, her way of making sense of the world. She had spent years chasing stories, filling notebooks with characters who felt more real to her than the people she met in everyday life. She wanted to be an author—not just someone who wrote in secret, but someone whose words left an imprint on the hearts of readers.

But dreams were fragile things, and publishing wasn't easy. She had faced rejection after rejection, each one a small crack in her confidence. Still, she wrote. Because she didn't know how to exist without it.

And tonight, she was on the verge of something—a scene, a chapter, maybe even an entire story—something that had been eluding her for days.

Her fingers tightened around her pen as she stared at the blank page. The words were there, just beneath the surface, but they refused to come.

And then, she felt it.

A presence.

Not loud or intrusive, but steady. Unignorable.

She glanced up, her gaze flickering toward the entrance.

Him.

Aarav hadn't planned to stay long.

Music had always been his language. He didn't need words the way writers did - he had chords, melodies, harmonies that spoke for him. But lately, even music had started feeling... hollow.

Back in Mumbai, he had been chasing the dream - open mics, underground gigs, anything that could get him noticed. And he had. His songs had started getting traction online. He had built a small but loyal following. A record label had even reached out, interested in his work.

But the pressure of turning passion into a profession had been suffocating. The music industry was ruthless, filled with expectations he wasn't sure he could meet. It had stopped being about the songs and started being about numbers—streams, views, followers.

So he had left. Not forever. Just for a while.

Manesar wasn't his final destination; it was a pause. A breath. A place to figure out if music was still his dream or if he had already lost it.

He had wandered into The Lantern Library out of curiosity, drawn by its quiet charm. And now, as he stood near the bookshelves, his eyes locked onto the girl by the stained-glass window.

Her.

He had noticed her the moment he walked in.

She wasn't just another face in the library - she was a presence. A force. The kind of person who carried stories in her eyes, who wrote like it was the only thing keeping her alive.

Aarav didn't believe in fate. But something about her made his fingers itch to pick up his guitar.

And without thinking, he moved closer.

Taarika was about to write her first sentence when a shadow fell over her notebook.

"Is this seat taken?"

The voice was low, warm, with a slight rasp—like someone who had spent too many nights singing in smoky rooms.

She looked up.

It was him.

Up close, she could see the faint stubble along his jawline, the ink smudges on his fingers, the tired intensity in his dark eyes.

He wasn't just handsome. He was... something else.

Something unfinished.

Taarika hesitated. She wasn't used to company when she wrote.

But instead of saying no, she heard herself say, "Go ahead."

Aarav slid into the chair across from her. He didn't open a book or take out his phone. Instead, he simply sat there, tracing invisible patterns on the wooden table, as if listening to something only he could hear.

Minutes passed in silence. Strangely, she didn't mind.

Then, without looking up, he said, "You write like you're running out of time."

Taarika's fingers stilled over her notebook.

"I write like I have something to say," she corrected.

A small smirk tugged at his lips. "Same thing, isn't it?"

She narrowed her eyes. "And you? You play music like it's the only thing keeping you alive?"

For a moment, something flickered in his gaze. Then, he leaned back, stretching his arms over his head. "Maybe. Or maybe I just like making noise."

Taarika huffed a quiet laugh. "That doesn't sound like a musician."

Aarav's smirk softened into something almost thoughtful. "And you don't sound like a writer."

Her brows lifted. "Excuse me?"

"I mean, you're not brooding, staring dramatically out the window, or carrying a typewriter around."

She scoffed. "Oh, so you believe in clichés?"

"Only the good ones," he said, grinning.

Taarika shook her head, but she was smiling now. She didn't know why she was still talking to him. She should've been annoyed. But somehow, this conversation felt effortless. Familiar, even.

Like a song she hadn't realized she knew the lyrics to.

Just then, a soft rumble of thunder echoed outside, making the stained-glass window tremble slightly. The rain had started.

Aarav glanced at the window and then back at her. "I don't believe in fate."

Taarika arched a brow. "Okay...?"

"But," he said, tapping his fingers against the table in a slow rhythm, "I do believe that some stories begin exactly when they're supposed to."

Something about the way he said it made her grip her pen tighter.

Maybe, just maybe, he was right.

3

Unwritten Melodies

The rain hadn't stopped since last evening. It drummed softly against the arched windows of "The Lantern Library", weaving its own quiet rhythm into the night.

Aarav sat at the same wooden table near the stained-glass window, fingers drumming absentmindedly on the surface. Across from him, Taarika flipped through the pages of an old poetry book, her pen occasionally tapping against the side of her notebook.

Neither of them spoke.

They didn't need to.

It had become a strange, unspoken routine - meeting here, sharing silences that felt heavier than words.

But tonight felt different.

Tonight, there was something lingering in the air, like a song waiting to be played.

Taarika stole a glance at him from behind her book.

Aarav had that faraway look in his eyes, the one she had started recognizing—the look of someone who had a melody stuck inside him, waiting to be let out.

She had watched him long enough to know the signs.

The way his fingers tapped against the table, like they were searching for invisible guitar strings.

The way he exhaled slowly, his lips parting just slightly as if he was humming a tune only he could hear.

The way his gaze flickered to his guitar case, lingering, hesitant.

She had never seen him play.

Not yet.

And that intrigued her more than she cared to admit.

She turned another page, pretending not to be invested. "You finally going to play something?"

Aarav blinked, snapping out of his thoughts. He smirked. "You sound like you've been waiting."

Taarika raised an eyebrow. "I haven't."

"You so have," he teased, leaning back in his chair. "You're dying of curiosity."

She rolled her eyes but didn't deny it. "So? Are you going to or not?"

Aarav hesitated. He wasn't sure why. He had played for hundreds of people before. Late-night gigs in Mumbai, college festivals, open mics. Music was second nature to him.

But this?

This felt different.

Because Taarika wasn't just another listener.

And that scared him.

Still, he reached for his guitar case, slowly unclipping the latches, the sound almost deafening in the quiet library.

Taarika leaned forward slightly, her usual guarded expression melting into something softer, something... expectant.

Aarav pulled out his guitar, running his fingers along the strings. The familiar feel of it steadied him.

He inhaled, then strummed.

The first chord was soft. Uncertain.

The second, smoother.

By the third, his eyes were closed, his fingers moving instinctively, pulling a melody from the silence.

Taarika's breath caught.

It was beautiful.

Not just the music, but the way he played—like the guitar wasn't just an instrument but a part of him. Like every note carried something unspoken, something too raw to be said out loud.

She let the sound wash over her, feeling it settle somewhere deep inside her chest.

And then, just as suddenly as he started, he stopped.

The silence that followed was almost jarring.

Taarika blinked, snapping out of the trance. "Why did you stop?"

Aarav exhaled, setting the guitar down. "Because it's not finished."

Taarika frowned. "What do you mean?"

Aarav looked down at the strings, his fingers tracing over them. "I've had this melody in my head for months. But I never figured out how to end it."

For a moment, she just watched him.

There was something in his voice-a hesitation, a wound left unspoken.

She didn't ask.

Instead, she picked up her pen, flipped to a blank page in her notebook, and after a brief pause, started writing.

Aarav frowned. "What are you doing?"

She looked up and smiled......a small, knowing smile. "Giving your song an ending."

Aarav stared at her, something shifting inside him.

She didn't pry. She didn't push.

She just understood.

And in that moment, as the rain whispered against the glass and her words bled onto paper, he realized.....

Maybe, just maybe, some stories weren't meant to be written alone.

4

Love Between the Lines

A week had passed since that night in The Lantern Library.

Since the song that wasn't finished. Since the words that lingered between them, unspoken yet undeniable.

And yet, every evening, they found themselves back at the same table-him with his guitar, her with her notebook—surrounded by books and a silence that wasn't really silence at all.

Aarav played. Taarika wrote.

Neither of them acknowledged the fact that their routine had started to feel... necessary.

But when the library closed for the night, when Taarika walked away with her notebook tucked under her arm, Aarav felt the absence of her presence more than he cared to admit.

That's when he did something he never thought he'd do.

He searched for her on Instagram.

....

Love Between the Lines! What It Means

Taarika had always believed that love wasn't just in grand declarations or poetic confessions. It was in the in-between moments.

It was in the spaces between words, in the pauses between sentences.

It was in the way someone looked at you when they thought you weren't watching. In the way someone remembered the little things-your favourite kind of tea, the way you hated writing with blue ink, the way you hummed to yourself when you were deep in thought.

Love wasn't just about the things people said.

It was about everything left unsaid.

It was written between the lines.

And somehow, she had started reading Aarav's story in those unspoken spaces.

In the way he played the same melody over and over, never quite finishing it.

In the way he stole glances at her when he thought she wasn't paying attention.

In the way his presence had started feeling like something permanent.

But permanence was a dangerous thing.

Because once you acknowledged it, you had to decide....did you run from it, or did you stay?

Taarika wasn't sure if she was ready for that choice.

....

Aarav's Late-Night Message

Aarav had never been the type to chase after someone.

But something about Taarika made him break all his own rules.

He found her Instagram account easily—@TaarikaWrites.

Her feed was a mixture of book quotes, writing snippets, and black-and-white photographs of places she had visited.

And then, there were her captions.

They weren't just words.

They were feelings.

"Some people enter your life like unfinished songs. You don't know how they end, but you keep listening anyway."

Aarav stared at the words longer than he should have, a strange feeling settling in his chest.

Without overthinking, he sent her a message.

Aarav: You always write this late? Or just when the words won't let you sleep?

The message was marked 'Seen' almost immediately.

His heart did something weird in his chest.

Then came her reply.

Taarika: Says the guy who's clearly awake and scrolling through my profile.

Aarav smirked. Busted.

Aarav: Guilty. But in my defense, I was just trying to find your number.

She took longer to reply this time.

Then

Taarika: And what makes you think I'd give it to you?

Aarav leaned back against his pillow, staring at his screen, fingers hovering over the keyboard.

Then, without hesitation, he typed:

Aarav: Because you already gave me your words. And I think you're curious about mine.

A long pause.

Maybe he had pushed too far.

Then

A notification.

A number.

He grinned.

....

The First Call That Changed Everything

That night, Aarav called her.

She picked up on the third ring. "I was just about to sleep, you know."

Aarav chuckled. "No, you weren't."

Taarika sighed, but he could hear the amusement in her voice. "You're impossible."

Aarav smirked. "I've been told."

A beat of silence.

Then, softer......

"Why did you really text me?"

Aarav hesitated, then said, "Because I think you and I are writing the same story. We just don't know how it ends yet."

Taarika's breath caught.

Because she knew, deep down—he wasn't just talking about words.

And for the first time in a long time, she wasn't sure if she wanted to edit the ending.

....

The Next Evening at the Library

The next evening, they met again at The Lantern Library.

Nothing had changed.

And yet, everything had.

Taarika noticed the way Aarav's eyes lingered on her just a second longer than usual.

Aarav noticed the way Taarika tucked her hair behind her ear, only to untuck it a moment later-nervous, uncertain.

They didn't talk about the messages. Or the phone call.

But they both felt it.

Something had shifted between them.

Aarav strummed his guitar absentmindedly, the same unfinished melody from before.

Taarika sighed, closing her notebook. "You really need to finish that song."

Aarav smirked. "You really need to let me read what you're writing."

She arched a brow. "Not a chance."

He chuckled. "Then we're at a stalemate."

Taarika bit her lip, thinking.

Then, slowly, she reached for his guitar. "Play something else."

Aarav raised an eyebrow. "Oh? Are you actually requesting a song?"

"Just play," she said, rolling her eyes.

Aarav exhaled, adjusted the guitar in his lap, and started playing a different melody-softer, slower.

Taarika closed her eyes.

And for the first time, she wasn't thinking about how the story would end.

She was just listening.

Because maybe, just maybe-

Love wasn't about the words.

It was about everything in between.

5

Threads of Fate

Aarav had spent the entire day debating whether to text her.

Sure, Taarika had given him her number. But did that mean she actually wanted him to use it?

By the time the sun dipped below the skyline, painting Manesar in hues of orange and purple, he finally gave in.

....

Aarav's Digital Pursuit

It started with Instagram.

Aarav scrolled through Taarika's profile for the third time that day. He had already gone through most of her posts, but somehow, he kept going back to them-her snippets of poetry, her black-and-white aesthetic, the rare candid photos of her sipping coffee, lost in thought.

He hesitated for only a second before hitting the Follow button.

Then, almost instinctively, he moved to Facebook.

Her profile was public, and as he scrolled through her old posts, he found himself smiling.

A book recommendation list that matched his taste.

A quote about music that made his chest tighten.

A picture of a library shelf, captioned: "Where words feel like home."

He hit Add Friend without overthinking.

Then, Twitter.

She wasn't overly active, but when she did tweet, it was either deep thoughts about writing or random things that made her laugh.

@AaravSings followed you.

He smirked, knowing she would see the notification.

And finally.......Hike and WhatsApp.

He had already saved her number, but now he updated her name in his contacts: Taarika (Writer Girl).

A moment later, a blue tick appeared on his screen.

She was online.

....

Taarika's Reaction

Taarika had just made herself a cup of coffee when her phone buzzed.

First, an Instagram notification. Then, Facebook. Then, Twitter.

Her row furrowed as she clicked through them, only to feel her stomach flip.

Aarav had followed her.

On everything.

She stared at her screen, her fingers hovering over the notification. She wasn't sure whether to be amused or exasperated.

Before she could process it, another notification popped up.

Aarav: You stalk me yet, or do I still have the upper hand?

She rolled her eyes but found herself smiling.

Taarika: You do realize following someone everywhere in one day is slightly concerning, right?

Aarav: It's research. Gotta understand my competition.

Taarika: Competition?

Aarav: Writers and musicians both tell stories. Just different mediums. I need to see if your words are as good as your attitude.

Taarika smirked, taking a sip of her coffee.

Taarika: So? Any verdict?

Aarav: Still undecided. Might have to read more.

Taarika sighed dramatically.

Taarika: Fine. Stalk away, musician.

Aarav grinned at his screen.

Aarav: Oh, I plan to.

......

An Unexpected Connection

Later that evening, Aarav's phone buzzed again.

It wasn't from Taarika this time.

It was from an old friend.

Riya: Dude. You know Taarika Sharma?

Aarav frowned at the message.

Aarav: Yeah?

Riya: She's my best friend.

Aarav blinked.

He hadn't expected that.

Before he could reply, his phone started ringing.

Riya's name flashed on the screen.

He answered instantly. "Wait.....how do you know her?"

Riya let out a laugh. "She's basically my sister. We've been best friends since forever. But HOW do YOU know her?"

Aarav hesitated, rubbing the back of his neck. "Met her at The Lantern Library. We've been... talking."

Riya gasped dramatically. "YOU? Talking to a writer? That's a plot twist."

Aarav chuckled. "What's that supposed to mean?"

"It means," Riya said, "that she's the type to get lost in books, and you're the type to get lost in songs. Opposites."

Aarav smirked. "Or two halves of the same story."

Riya paused. "Oh, wow. That was poetic. You're already under her influence."

Aarav rolled his eyes. "You're overreacting."

"Am I?" Riya teased. "Because Taarika never gives guys the time of day. If she's talking to you, she's at least curious."

Aarav leaned back, letting her words settle.

Curious.

That was a good start.

....

Taarika's Side of the Story

Meanwhile, at her apartment, Taarika's phone buzzed again.

Riya: TAARIKA. EXPLAIN.

Taarika groaned, already knowing what was coming.

She sighed and called her. "Before you say anything—"

"Oh no, NO. We are NOT skipping past this," Riya interrupted. "YOU and Aarav? The musician?"

Taarika exhaled. "We're just... talking."

Riya let out a dramatic gasp. "Talking leads to things, Taarika."

Taarika rolled her eyes. "It's not a love story."

Riya was grinning on the other end. "Not yet."

Taarika groaned, flopping onto her bed. "I should never have introduced you to romance novels."

Riya laughed. "Too late."

Taarika bit her lip, staring at her ceiling. "He's different, though."

"Oh?"

"He's not trying too hard. He's not pretending. He just... is."

\+ 6999999999999999999Riya softened. "And you like that?"

Taarika hesitated. "I don't know."

But deep down, maybe she did.

Maybe she was starting to read between the lines of their story.

And maybe, just maybe....she wanted to see where it led.

....

The Next Day......A Chance Encounter

The next evening, as Taarika walked into The Lantern Library, her phone vibrated.

Aarav: Look up.

She frowned, glancing around.

And then, she saw him.

Aarav, leaning against a bookshelf, smirking at her.

Taarika rolled her eyes but couldn't fight the small smile playing at her lips.

He walked over, casually slipping his hands into his pockets. "Miss me?"

She huffed a laugh. "You're ridiculous."

Aarav grinned. "And you're pretending you weren't looking for me."

She stared at him for a second, then shook her head, amused. "You wish, musician."

He chuckled. "Maybe."

And just like that, they slipped into conversation, their usual rhythm of banter and teasing, completely unaware that the invisible thread of fate between them had just grown stronger.

6

When Silence Speaks

Aarav had never been good with words.

He could string together melodies that spoke of love, longing, and heartbreak, but when it came to saying how he felt...really felt....he always fell short.

So, he did the only thing he knew how to do.

He wrote a song.

....

Aarav's Late-Night Confession

It had started as a simple melody.

A few soft chords played absentmindedly in his dimly lit room, the familiar hum of his guitar filling the quiet space. He hadn't planned to write a song about her.

But then, he never planned on meeting someone like Taarika either.

His fingers moved on instinct, plucking out notes that felt like memories.

The way she furrowed her brows when she was lost in thought.

The way she pretended not to care when she clearly did.

The way her words...effortless, beautiful....had started creeping into his own thoughts.

Before he knew it, the lyrics were forming in his head.

He grabbed a pen.

And he let the song write itself.

....

Taarika's Restless Night

Taarika couldn't sleep.

Her mind kept going back to him.

To the way his voice dipped lower when he was teasing her.

To the way his fingers absentmindedly tapped out rhythms when he was thinking.

To the way he looked at her sometimes, like he was seeing something worth writing about.

She shook her head. No.

This wasn't supposed to happen.

Aarav was a musician. Musicians left. They chased dreams bigger than people, bigger than moments.

And yet, there was something about him.....something that made her heart race in ways she wasn't ready to admit.

She sighed, rolling onto her side and grabbing her phone.

That's when she saw it.

A message from Aarav.

Aarav: Check YouTube.

Her brow furrowed.

Curious, she clicked the link he sent.

A video popped up.

It was him.

Sitting on his rooftop, guitar in hand, the Manesar skyline glowing behind him.

The title?

"When Silence Speaks ...... An Unfinished Love Song."

Her breath hitched.

Taarika hesitated for only a moment before pressing play.

....

The Song That Said Everything

The moment his fingers touched the strings, she felt it.

A pull. Deep and undeniable.

The melody was soft, almost hesitant at first, but then it grew, filled with something raw and real.

Then, his voice....low, aching, unguarded.....wrapped around the lyrics like a confession.

"She writes in whispers, in unsaid dreams,

Spilling love between the lines unseen.

And I play the notes she'll never hear,

A song meant only for her ears..."

Taarika's breath caught.

The lyrics. The way he sang them.

The way his voice wove through the melody like something unfinished, something still waiting for an answer.

This wasn't just any song.

This was for her.

Her chest tightened as she scrolled through the comments.

@MiraWrites: "This feels like an unsaid love story. Who's the lucky girl?"

@AshGuitarist: "Bro, this is deep. If she doesn't get the hint, I will cry for you."

@LyricalSoul: "This isn't just a song. This is a silent proposal."

Taarika's fingers trembled as she refreshed the page.

The views were skyrocketing.

People were sharing it, calling it the most heartbreakingly beautiful love song of the year.

And suddenly, she felt breathless.

She closed her eyes, trying to steady her thoughts.

Aarav had always hidden behind his music. But this?

This wasn't hiding.

This was a confession.

A silent, aching, indirect proposal.

And the worst part?

She wasn't sure if she was ready to hear it.

....

The Next Morning.......Aarav's Expectation vs. Reality

Aarav woke up to his phone buzzing like crazy.

Hundreds of notifications. His song had gone viral overnight.

Messages poured in. Old friends. Random followers. Even people from his past who suddenly wanted to reconnect.

But the only message he was waiting for never came.

Not from her.

Not a single word from Taarika.

He checked their last chat.

Aarav: Check YouTube.

Taarika: Seen 2:13 AM.

That was it.

A sinking feeling settled in his chest.

Maybe he had misread everything. Maybe this was one-sided. Maybe—

His phone buzzed.

Taarika: Meet me at The Lantern Library. 5 PM.

Aarav exhaled, running a hand through his hair.

So, she had heard him.

Now the only question was.........

Would she finally say something back?

....

The Meeting That Changed Everything

Taarika sat at their usual table, fingers wrapped around a warm cup of coffee, heart pounding in a way she couldn't control.

The song was still stuck in her head.

Aarav's voice. His words. His feelings.

She didn't know what to say to him.

But when the door creaked open and he walked in, looking at her like she already knew...

She realized she didn't have to say anything.

Because love wasn't always in the words.

Sometimes, love was in the silences.

And as Aarav sat across from her, waiting, searching her face for an answer, she knew........

This was just the beginning.

7
The Fear of Falling

Taarika had always believed in love.

Not the fairytale kind, not the grand, cinematic declarations. She believed in the quiet kind.....the love that existed in stolen glances, in shared silences, in the spaces between words.

But belief was one thing. Accepting it was another.

And right now, as she sat across from Aarav at The Lantern Library, his song still playing in her mind, she was terrified.

....

Unspoken Feelings and a Lingering Song

Since the moment she heard Aarav's song, something had shifted.

She had always known there was something between them. But now? Now it had a melody. A voice. A weight.

And that weight sat between them, heavy and unspoken.

She sipped her coffee, trying to act normal. "Your song is... nice."

Aarav raised an eyebrow. "Nice?"

Taarika avoided his gaze. "Yeah."

He smirked. "Wow. I pour my heart out, and all I get is nice?"

She fought a smile. "What do you want me to say?"

Aarav leaned in slightly, eyes locked on hers. "That you heard it."

Taarika exhaled. Of course, she had heard it.

She had felt it in her bones.

But saying that out loud? That was dangerous.

She put her cup down. "It's just a song, Aarav."

He stared at her for a moment, then leaned back, an unreadable expression on his face. "If you say so."

But she didn't miss the flicker of disappointment in his eyes.

And it made something in her chest ache.

....

Aarav's Frustration.......And a Hint of Jealousy

Later that evening, Aarav found himself at Caffeine &
Chapters, the café near the library. He wasn't in the mood
for coffee, but he needed to clear his head.

She was running.

He had bared his soul in a song, and she had brushed
it off like it was nothing.

And yet........he couldn't be mad.

Because deep down, he knew why.

Taarika was afraid.

Afraid of how real this was becoming. Afraid that
choosing him meant risking something she wasn't ready
to lose.

Lost in thought, he didn't realize someone had walked
up beside him.

"Hey, stranger."

Aarav glanced up.

Ishaan.

Taarika's friend.

And the moment Aarav saw him, irritation pricked at
the edges of his mind.

Because Ishaan wasn't just any friend. He was the kind
of guy who had always been around Taarika, the one who
made her laugh too easily, the one who knew her far

longer than Aarav did.

And right now? Right now, he was sitting across from her, laughing over something, their heads tilted toward each other.

Aarav clenched his jaw.

He had no right to be jealous.

But damn if he didn't hate the way Ishaan looked at her.

Like he had a chance.

Like he didn't know that Taarika already had a song written about her.

Aarav tapped his fingers against the table, trying to drown out the irrational annoyance brewing inside him.

Until Ishaan's voice cut through.

"So, Taarika.......when are you going to let me read your new story?"

Aarav's eyes snapped to Taarika.

She let him read her writing?

That stung.

Taarika hesitated, glancing at Aarav for the briefest second before turning back to Ishaan. "It's not finished yet."

Ishaan grinned. "That's fine. I just want to be the first to read it."

Aarav let out a short laugh before he could stop himself.

Both Ishaan and Taarika turned to look at him.

Aarav shrugged, picking up his coffee. "Funny. She won't even let me see what she's working on."

Ishaan chuckled. "Maybe because I don't annoy her 24/ 7."

Aarav smirked, but his eyes stayed on Taarika. "Or maybe because she's afraid I'll find myself in her pages."

Taarika stiffened.

Aarav saw it........the slight shift, the way her fingers tightened around her cup.

And suddenly, he knew.

She had written about him.

....

A Confrontation Under the Stars

Later that night, after Ishaan left and the café was closing, Aarav followed Taarika outside.

The air was crisp, the streets quieter than usual.

"Taarika."

She stopped but didn't turn around.

Aarav sighed, shoving his hands into his jacket pockets. "Just tell me the truth."

She exhaled. "About what?"

His voice softened. "About why you're running from this."

Taarika finally turned to face him. "I'm not running."

Aarav stepped closer. "Then why won't you let me read your writing?"

She hesitated.

He tilted his head, eyes searching hers. "Because you have written about me, haven't you?"

Taarika swallowed hard. "That's not the point."

Aarav took another step closer. "Then what is the point?"

Silence.

Then..........

She whispered, "I don't want to ruin this."

Aarav's chest tightened.

"Taarika..." He took her hand gently, his thumb brushing against her palm. "You won't."

She looked up at him, eyes filled with something raw, something vulnerable.

And for the first time, she let herself feel it.

The warmth of his touch. The way his presence steadied her.

The way falling for him wasn't just inevitable.......it had already happened.

And maybe.....just maybe.....she didn't have to be afraid anymore.

8

A Fear We Can't Name

Love was supposed to be beautiful.

That's what all the stories said.

But what the stories didn't talk about was fear.

The kind that crept in when things started feeling too real. The kind that made you second-guess every look, every touch, every unspoken word.

And right now, that fear was settling between Taarika and Aarav, thick and heavy—like an unfinished sentence waiting for an ending.

....

The Distance That Wasn't There Before

Over the past few days, something had changed between them.

Aarav still came to The Lantern Library.

Taarika still sat across from him.

Their usual banter still happened.

But there was a weight in their silences now.

A hesitation in the way she looked at him.

A flicker of uncertainty in the way he touched his guitar, as if he wasn't sure if playing for her still meant the same thing.

Aarav felt it.

And it was driving him insane.

One night, after they finished their usual coffee at Caffeine & Chapters, Aarav finally snapped.

"Are you going to tell me what's going on?"

Taarika blinked. "What?"

Aarav crossed his arms, his gaze steady. "You're avoiding something. And I don't think it's me. I think it's this." He gestured between them.

She looked away. "You're overthinking."

Aarav let out a dry laugh. "Am I?"

Taarika pressed her lips together, gripping her cup tightly.

Aarav sighed, running a hand through his hair. "You're pulling away."

Taarika flinched. "I'm not..."

"You are," he cut in, voice softer now. "And I need to know why."

Her heart pounded. Because you're making me feel things I can't afford to feel.

Because if she let herself love him, it wouldn't be something small. It wouldn't be something she could walk away from.

It would be everything.

And that terrified her.

So she said nothing.

Aarav watched her for a long moment, then nodded slowly, like he understood.

Like he already knew what she wasn't saying.

"Okay," he murmured, stepping back. "If that's how you want it."

Then, without another word, he turned and walked away.

And Taarika let him.

Even though every part of her was screaming at her not to.

....

Aarav's Silent Heartbreak

Aarav didn't go to the library the next day.

Distance wasn't always measured in miles.

Sometimes, it was in unsent texts, in stolen glances that didn't meet, in words left hanging between two people who once knew how to fill the silence.

And right now, there was more distance between Aarav and Taarika than ever before.

....

Aarav's Absence

For the first time since they met, Aarav didn't show up at The Lantern Library.

Or Caffeine & Chapters.

Or anywhere she had grown used to finding him.

Taarika told herself she was fine with it.

She wanted space.

She needed to sort out her thoughts, to figure out what she really wanted.

But by the third day without a single message, she realized something.....

She missed him.

She missed his sarcastic remarks, the way he strummed absentmindedly on his guitar while she wrote. The way he looked at her, like she was the only thing worth paying attention to in a room full of people.

And now, all of it was gone.

Because of her.

Because she was too scared to admit what was right in front of her.

She stared at her phone for what felt like the hundredth time that day.

9
The Distance Between Us

No new messages.

Her fingers hovered over the keyboard, hesitating.

But what would she even say?

Would he even reply?

Before she could decide, her phone buzzed.

Not a text.

Not a call.

A notification.

Aarav had posted on Instagram.

And when she clicked on it, her breath caught.

It was a video.

A black-and-white clip of him sitting on his rooftop, guitar in hand, the city lights flickering behind him.

No caption.

No words.

Just music.

She hit play, and the first few chords were enough to make her chest tighten.

It was their melody.

The unfinished song.

The one he had played for her in the library.

Only now, it sounded different.

Sadder.

Like he had finally found an ending, and she wasn't sure if she wanted to hear it.

....

Taarika's Breaking Point

That night, she couldn't sleep.

Aarav's song played on a loop in her mind, every note a reminder of what she was trying so hard to avoid.

At 2:17 AM, she finally gave in.

She grabbed her phone and did something she hadn't done in days.

She called him.

The phone rang once.

Twice.

Three times.

Then...

It went to voicemail.

Taarika's stomach sank.

She swallowed, staring at the screen, before whispering, "I miss you."

Then, before she could overthink it, she hung up.

And hoped he had heard her.

.....

Aarav's Silence

The next day, there was still no reply.

Taarika walked into The Lantern Library, half-expecting to see him sitting at their usual table, waiting with that knowing smirk.

But the seat was empty.

For the first time since she had met him, it hit her.....

What if he didn't come back?

What if she had pushed him too far?

She exhaled shakily, dropping into her chair and burying her face in her hands.

This wasn't how their story was supposed to go.

She had spent so long running from the possibility of losing him that she never realized......

She had already lost him.

And maybe, this time, it wasn't up to him to fix it.

Maybe it was her turn to fight for what they had.

10
The Surprise for Taarika

Taarika had no idea where she was going.

Her friends had planned a surprise get-together, and she had agreed without asking too many questions. It had been days since she had properly gone out, her mind a mess of unsaid words and unresolved feelings. Maybe a distraction was exactly what she needed.

But the moment she stepped through the door, her breath hitched.

This wasn't just any house.

It was Aarav's house.

Her heartbeat faltered as she looked around—the warm, welcoming space, the framed pictures of a younger Aarav with his family, the unmistakable scent of something homely.

Before she could react, an older woman with kind eyes and a warm smile approached her.

"You must be Taarika," the woman said, beaming. "I've heard so much about you."

Taarika blinked in surprise. "You have?"

Aarav's mother laughed, leading her inside. "Oh, of course! Aarav talks about you all the time. And after seeing you, I understand why."

Heat rushed to Taarika's cheeks. He talks about me?

Before she could process that, Aarav's father joined them, clapping her lightly on the back. "So, you're the writer, huh? The one who's always stealing our son's attention."

Taarika let out a nervous laugh. "I... I wouldn't say that."

Aarav's mom exchanged a knowing glance with her husband before looking at Taarika fondly. "You know, he never let anyone read his lyrics before. Not even us. But with you, it's different."

Taarika's chest tightened. Different.

The more she spoke to Aarav's parents, the more she saw the little things about him that she had never known.

How he always woke up early on Sundays just to make chai for his mom.

How he kept an old, tattered notebook full of unfinished songs that no one was allowed to touch.

How he pretended to hate romantic movies but secretly enjoyed them.

Every little thing they shared made her fall deeper.

By the time the evening was coming to an end, she had made up her mind.

She was done running.

She was ready to say yes.

But just as she turned to find Aarav, she heard a voice behind her.

"Aarav's changed a lot since his breakup, hasn't he?"

Taarika froze.

She turned slowly, finding Aarav's brother standing beside her, casually sipping his drink.

Her throat tightened. "Breakup?"

Aarav's brother raised an eyebrow. "You didn't know?" He let out a small chuckle. "Yeah, it was bad. He doesn't talk about it much, but it took him a long time to move on."

Taarika felt like the air had been knocked out of her lungs.

Aarav had been in love before. He had been heartbroken before.

And now, all the words she had planned to say to him felt like they didn't matter anymore.

Maybe she wasn't special. Maybe she was just another chapter in his story.

And suddenly, she wasn't sure if she could handle that.

11

A Love She Never Knew

Taarika had always believed that time healed everything.

But weeks passed, and she called Aarav's brother for his breakup reason.

he said casually. "His last relationship messed him up pretty bad."

Taarika stilled. "What's her name?"

Aarav's brother sighed. "Her name was Mebi. They were together for almost two years."

Taarika tried to keep her tone neutral.

A bitter truth....

"She liked the idea of Aarav more than she liked him. She loved the musician, not the man. As long as he was writing songs about her, playing to make her feel special, she adored him. But the moment he talked about his real dreams....about teaching music, about writing songs that weren't about her....she lost interest."

Taarika's stomach twisted. "She didn't support him?"

"Support?" His brother scoffed. "She told him he wasn't good enough to make it big. That if he ever stopped writing about her, no one would listen to his songs."

Taarika felt a wave of anger rise in her chest. How could anyone say that to him?

"But the worst part?" His brother's voice lowered. "She was cheating on him for months. And Aarav knew."

Taarika's breath caught. "He... knew?"

"He found out early on. But he still tried to make it work. Thought he could fix things, that maybe it was just a mistake."

Taarika swallowed the lump in her throat. Aarav had loved her. Truly.

"So what changed?" she whispered.

His brother narrated. "One night, he went to surprise her. But when he got there, he saw her with someone else. And when she saw him?"

He shook his head. "She didn't even look guilty. Just told him that she was 'bored' of their relationship."

Taarika's hands curled into fists. How could someone be so cruel?

"And you know what hurt him the most?" His brother exhaled. "She said she only dated him because musicians make great love stories."

Taarika felt like she was going to be sick.

She had used him. Played with his heart like he was just another song to be written and forgotten.

And suddenly, everything made sense.

The way Aarav hesitated to trust.

The way he never talked about his past.

The way he always seemed like he was holding something back.

Because he had been burned before.

Because he had given his heart away once... and it had been crushed.

And now?

Taarika was afraid he wouldn't let her in.

Not after what he had been through.

....

A Love Story Waiting to Be Written

Taarika walked home that night with a storm raging in her chest.

She wanted to hate Mebi.

But more than that... she wanted to prove that she wasn't like her.

That she saw Aarav. Not just the musician. Not just the boy who wrote beautiful songs.

She saw the man behind the lyrics.

And she loved him for it.

But when she finally decided to tell him...

She wasn't sure if he would still be willing to listen.

12
The Echo of His Words

Taarika had never been afraid of words.

Words had always been her home, her escape, her way of making sense of the world.

But his words?

They haunted her.

"I love you. I don't know how to stop."

She had waited so long to hear them. And yet, when they finally came, they terrified her.

Because love...real love...wasn't just something you felt. It was something you chose.

And she wasn't sure if she was brave enough to choose it.

Not when she knew love could also mean heartbreak.

....

Avoidance and Unspoken Longing

For days after that night, she avoided him.

Not intentionally.

Or maybe exactly that.

She stayed away from The Lantern Library, choosing to work from home instead. She ignored the way her fingers hovered over his name in her contacts.

She wasn't ready.

But what she didn't know was that Aarav was waiting.

Waiting for her to come back.

Waiting for her to say something.

Waiting for her to prove that he hadn't imagined what was between them.

And when she didn't?

Aarav did something he swore he wouldn't.

He went looking for her.

....

Aarav's Search for Taarika

Aarav hadn't meant to show up at Caffeine & Chapters.

But as he pushed open the door, scanning the café, he felt something deep in his chest......hope and disappointment tangled together.

She wasn't there.

His fingers tightened around his phone. He could text her. Call her.

But if she wanted to talk to him, she would have already.

And that realization? It made his heart ache in a way he wasn't prepared for.

"Waiting for someone?"

Aarav turned to see Riya, leaning against the counter, watching him with a knowing smirk.

He sighed. "What gave it away?"

Riya chuckled. "You only ever look that restless when it comes to Taarika."

He ran a hand through his hair. "She's avoiding me."

Riya's smile faded. "You told her, didn't you?"

Aarav nodded. "Yeah."

"And?"

"And then she disappeared."

Riya sighed, crossing her arms. "That sounds like Taarika."

Aarav frowned. "What does that mean?"

Riya hesitated. "She's scared. She doesn't do love easily. She overthinks, second-guesses, convinces herself it's better not to risk it. And you? You're not just some random guy to her, Aarav. You matter."

Aarav exhaled sharply. "Then why does it feel like I don't?"

Riya gave him a small, sad smile. "Because when something means this much, running away feels safer than staying."

Aarav's jaw tightened.

He wasn't going to be another thing she ran from.

,,,,,,,,,,,,,,,,,,,,,,

Taarika's Turmoil

Taarika sat on her bed, staring at her phone.

Riya had just texted her.

Riya: Aarav came looking for you.

Her stomach twisted.

Of course, he did.

Because he felt things without hesitation. Loved without conditions.

And she?

She didn't know how to let herself do the same.

She exhaled shakily, her fingers tightening around her phone.

And then, before she could stop herself, she did something reckless.

She searched Aarav's name on YouTube.

The first video that popped up made her breath hitch.

"A Love She Never Knew – An Unfinished Song."

Her hands trembled as she clicked play.

....

A Song Meant for Her

The video was simple.

Aarav. Sitting on the rooftop. Guitar in hand. The city glowing behind him.

And then....his voice.

"She's the kind of love that leaves ink on your fingertips,

A story written in stolen glances and missed chances."

Taarika swallowed hard.

"She doesn't know she's a song waiting to be sung,

She doesn't know I already hear the melody."

Her chest tightened.

"And maybe she's afraid to love me back,

Maybe she's afraid I'll leave."

Tears pricked at her eyes.

"But love like this"

His voice broke slightly on the last line.

"Love like this doesn't walk away."

Taarika covered her mouth, emotions overwhelming her.

He was waiting.

Still.

Despite everything.

And suddenly, she knew.

If she didn't go to him now...if she let this moment slip away...she would regret it forever.

....

The Rain-Soaked Realization

Taarika didn't remember grabbing her coat.

Didn't remember running down the streets of Manesar.

All she knew was that she needed to find him.

The rain started falling as she reached his apartment building.

She knocked once.

Twice.

Then the door swung open.

Aarav.

Wet hair. Barefoot. Heart in his eyes.

Neither of them spoke.

And then...........

Taarika stepped forward and threw her arms around him.

Aarav stiffened for half a second.

Then, without hesitation, he held her back.

Tightly.

Like she was something worth holding on to.

Like she was his.

The rain poured around them, but neither of them cared.

Because finally, finally........

She had stopped running.

13

The Love That Wasn't

The Fear of Loving Someone Who Could Leave

Taarika had always believed in love.

At least, she thought she did.

But then why did it feel like she was walking on the edge of something dangerous?

She had felt safe before Aarav. Comfortable in her own world, where love existed in stories but didn't demand to be real.

Now, love was real.

And it was terrifying.

Because what if she loved him only for him to leave?

What if he became another name in a list of people who had promised forever but never stayed?

And worst of all.......

What if she wasn't enough to make him stay?

....

The Past That Still Haunted Aarav

Aarav knew something was wrong the moment Taarika pulled away again.

It wasn't obvious at first. She still met him at The Lantern Library, still listened when he played, still smiled at his jokes.

But something had changed.

Her laughs didn't linger as long.

Her eyes didn't hold his the way they used to.

She was present, but it felt like a version of her was missing.

And he had no idea how to fix it.

Then, one evening, he found his answer.

Or rather.....his past found her.

....

A Meeting That Changed Everything

Taarika hadn't planned on staying at Caffeine & Chapters that night.

She had stopped in for a quick coffee, needing a break from her tangled thoughts.

And that's when she heard her name.

"Taarika Sharma?"

She turned, only to find herself face to face with a woman she had never met.

But the moment she saw her, she knew.

Mebi.

Aarav's ex.

Tall. Confident. The kind of woman who looked like she had never been uncertain a day in her life.

And suddenly, Taarika felt small.

Mebi gave her a once-over, then smiled—a little too knowing, a little too sharp.

"So," Mebi mused, stirring her coffee, "you're the one."

Taarika frowned. "Excuse me?"

"The girl Aarav wrote his new songs about."

Her stomach twisted. "I don't know what you're talking about."

Mebi chuckled, shaking her head. "Of course you do."

Taarika didn't reply.

Because she did know.

And Mebi knew she knew.

Which made this conversation infinitely worse.

Mebi leaned forward slightly. "Has he told you?"

"Told me what?"

"About us."

Taarika's fingers clenched around her cup. "I know you were together."

Mebi smirked. "Did he tell you how it ended?"

Silence.

And there it was.

The moment the past threatened to rewrite the present.

Mebi tilted her head, watching her. "Let me guess. He's amazing, right? Plays you songs that make you feel like you're the only person in the world?"

Taarika swallowed hard.

Mebi sighed, as if this was a conversation she had had before. "And then, just when you think you finally have him... something changes."

Taarika's heart pounded. "What are you trying to say?"

Mebi tapped her nails against the table. "That I've seen this story before. I've lived it."

Taarika shook her head. "Aarav isn't like that."

Mebi smiled, but it wasn't warm. "That's what I thought, too."

Taarika's breath caught.

And suddenly, doubt settled into her chest.

....

Aarav's Side of the Story

When Aarav walked into Caffeine & Chapters later that night, he felt it immediately.......

Something was wrong.

Taarika was sitting alone, staring at her coffee like it had personally betrayed her.

His stomach twisted.

"Taarika?"

She looked up at him, her expression unreadable. "Did you love her?"

Aarav stilled.

She didn't have to say who. He already knew.

Aarav exhaled, pulling out the chair across from her. "I thought I did."

Taarika's fingers trembled slightly. "And yet, she's the one telling me how our story ends."

His heart sank. "She talked to you."

Taarika nodded. "She said she's seen this before. That she was me."

Aarav clenched his jaw. "It's not the same."

"Then tell me how it's different."

Silence.

Aarav ran a hand through his hair. "Mebi and I... we weren't right for each other. I was young, and I mistook comfort for love. I thought we had something real, but........."

"But?"

Aarav's gaze met hers, raw and unguarded.

"She left before I could."

Taarika inhaled sharply.

"She broke up with me first," Aarav admitted, voice quieter now. "Because she knew I wasn't all in."

Taarika swallowed hard. "And with me? Are you all in?"

Aarav didn't hesitate.

"Yes."

Taarika wanted to believe him.

But Mebi's words echoed in her mind.

"And then, just when you think you finally have him... something changes."

What if Mebi was right?

What if she was just another name in Aarav's past, waiting to happen?

Aarav's voice softened. "Taarika, please don't let her past with me ruin our present."

Taarika exhaled shakily. "I don't know how to stop being afraid."

Aarav reached for her hand, fingers curling gently around hers.

"Then let me prove to you that you don't have to be."

Taarika looked at him.

And for the first time, she wanted to believe him.

But fear?

Fear had a way of whispering louder than love.

14
The Truth Between the Chords

The Song That Said Everything

Aarav had always believed that music could say what words couldn't.

That's why he wrote.

Because sometimes, love wasn't something you could just say.

It was something you had to feel.

And tonight, he was going to make Taarika feel it.

....

Aarav's Surprise Performance

The café was buzzing with quiet chatter as the open mic night continued.

Taarika sat in the back, her fingers tracing the rim of her coffee cup, heart unsettled.

She hadn't planned on coming. Not after the conversation with Mebi. Not after the doubts had settled in her chest like a storm waiting to break.

But then Riya had dragged her here.

"Just listen to him, Taarika," Riya had said. "If you walk away after this, fine. But don't run before you know."

So now, she was here.

And then......

The room hushed as Aarav stepped onto the stage.

Taarika froze.

His guitar was slung across his shoulder, the dim lights casting shadows across his face.

But it was his eyes that made her breath catch.

Because when he looked at her....across the crowded café, across the space that had grown between them......he looked like a man who had something to prove.

A slow, soft strum of his guitar filled the silence.

Then, he began to sing.

"She doesn't see the way the world slows down when she walks in,"

"She doesn't hear the way her silence is louder than any sound."

Taarika's fingers tightened around her cup.

"She doesn't know that she's in every song I play,"

"That I don't have the words, but I still find ways to say…"

Aarav's voice softened, and in that moment, it was just them.

"That I love her.

In the way I wait for her, even when she's not coming."

In the way I write her into songs she'll never hear."

"In the way I hold my breath… every time she leaves."

The room blurred.

Taarika's heart pounded so hard she was sure everyone could hear it.

And when Aarav reached the last line, his voice was barely more than a whisper……

"But maybe, if she listens… she'll finally know."

Silence.

Thick. Heavy.

Then, applause erupted.

But Taarika didn't hear it.

Because all she could hear was him.

And the truth between the chords.

....

The Moment That Changed Everything

Taarika didn't remember standing up.

Didn't remember moving.

All she knew was that one second, she was sitting in the back of the café—

And the next, she was walking straight toward him.

Aarav was stepping off the stage when she reached him.

"Taarika......."

She didn't let him finish.

Before she could lose her nerve, she grabbed his shirt, pulled him down—

And kissed him.

Aarav sucked in a sharp breath against her lips, but then—

Then he was kissing her back.

Like he had been waiting for this.

Like she had been waiting for this.

The café blurred. The people disappeared.

It was just him. His hands gripping her waist, pulling her closer. His lips moving against hers, slow and careful, like he was memorizing the way she felt.

When they finally broke apart, their breaths were uneven.

Aarav stared at her, his forehead resting against hers.

"I wasn't sure if you'd listen," he whispered.

Taarika exhaled shakily. "I wasn't sure if I was ready."

Aarav smiled, brushing a strand of hair from her face. "And now?"

Taarika bit her lip, eyes searching his.

Then, softly.......

"Play it for me again."

Aarav's heart skipped a beat.

And in that moment, he knew.

She wasn't running anymore.

15

If We're Honest

The Aftermath of the Kiss

Aarav had kissed a lot of people before.

But never like this.

Never like his heart was on the line.

Never like he was afraid that if he pulled away, the moment would slip through his fingers.

But the moment did end.

Because the second their lips parted, Taarika stepped back.

And just like that, reality rushed in.

The café. The people watching. The weight of what had just happened.

Aarav swallowed hard. "Taarika?"

She looked at him, breathless, eyes wide, as if she wasn't sure if what had just happened was real.

Then, without a word.......

She turned and walked away.

....

The Conversation They Couldn't Avoid

Aarav found her hours later.

Sitting on the rooftop of The Lantern Library, knees pulled to her chest, staring at the dark sky as if it held answers.

"Taarika."

She didn't look at him. "I shouldn't have kissed you."

Aarav's heart clenched. "Do you regret it?"

She was quiet for a long moment. Then—

"No."

Relief flooded through him.

But before he could say anything, she turned to face him, eyes uncertain. "But I'm scared."

Aarav sat down beside her, leaving just enough space between them. "Of what?"

She exhaled, hugging her knees. "Of how much this matters."

Aarav understood.

Because it scared him too.

"I don't want to lose you," she admitted softly.

Aarav looked at her. "Then don't."

She turned to him, eyes vulnerable. "It's not that simple."

Aarav gave a small smile. "Maybe it is."

Taarika hesitated. "You say that now. But what if things get complicated? What if we don't work? What if……."

Aarav reached for her hand, threading his fingers through hers.

"We don't get to know the ending before we start, Taarika."

She swallowed hard. "But what if I'm not ready?"

Aarav squeezed her hand gently. "Then I'll wait."

Taarika's eyes softened.

And for the first time, she started to believe that maybe...just maybe....this didn't have to end in heartbreak.

16
A Heart That Can't Let Go

Aarav's Choice

For the first time in his life, Aarav had to choose between love and music.

A record label in Mumbai had seen his viral song. They wanted to meet him.

This was everything he had worked for.

But all he could think about was her.

Taarika.

The girl who had made him believe in stories again. The girl who had turned his unfinished melodies into something real.

And suddenly, he wasn't sure if music meant as much without her.

....

The Call That Changed Everything

Taarika's phone buzzed.

Aarav: Can we meet?

She hesitated. Then—

Taarika: Where?

Five minutes later, she was standing outside Caffeine & Chapters, heart racing as Aarav walked up to her.

There was something different about him tonight.

A hesitation. A weight in his eyes.

"What's wrong?" she asked.

Aarav ran a hand through his hair. "I got an offer."

Taarika's stomach twisted. "For what?"

"A music contract."

She swallowed. "That's... amazing."

Aarav hesitated. "It's in Mumbai."

Silence.

Taarika's heart ached. She knew this was his dream.

But why did it feel like a goodbye?

"When do you leave?" she asked quietly.

Aarav looked at her. "I haven't decided if I'm going yet."

Taarika's breath caught. "Why not?"

He stepped closer, voice softer. "Because of you."

Taarika's eyes widened. "Aarav…"

He exhaled. "Tell me to stay, and I will."

Her throat tightened. "I can't do that."

Aarav's jaw clenched. "Why not?"

"Because this is your dream," she whispered. "I won't be the reason you don't chase it."

Aarav stared at her for a long moment.

Then, finally, he nodded.

And it broke her.

Because he wasn't fighting.

He was accepting it.

And maybe… that hurt even more.

....

The Goodbye That Wasn't Goodbye

That night, Taarika sat on her bed, staring at her phone.

She wanted to call him.

Wanted to tell him to stay.

But she couldn't.

Because love wasn't about holding someone back.

It was about letting them fly.

Her phone buzzed.

Aarav: I'll wait for you.

Taarika closed her eyes, tears slipping down her cheeks.

And for the first time, she realized—

Maybe love wasn't about choosing between dreams.

Maybe love was about finding a way back to each other.

No matter how far they went.

17
The Spaces Between Us

The Silence That Said Everything

Distance wasn't just measured in miles.

It was measured in silence.

It had been three weeks since Aarav left for Mumbai. Three weeks since he walked away from Caffeine & Chapters with a promise that he would wait for her.

Taarika had been convincing herself that she was fine. That she had made the right decision.

But then why did her world feel... quieter?

....

Aarav's Life in Mumbai

Mumbai was loud.

Everything moved too fast. The music industry was ruthless, filled with people who wanted numbers, not art.

Aarav should have been happy.

His songs were being recorded. His name was starting to mean something.

But every time he played his guitar, every time he wrote new lyrics, all he could think about was her.

Taarika.

The girl who had once sat across from him in The Lantern Library, listening to his unfinished melodies like they were the only thing that mattered.

And now?

Now, she was a silence he couldn't escape.

....

Taarika's Writing Blogs

Taarika had always found comfort in words.

But now, the words refused to come.

Every time she tried to write, she ended up staring at a blank page, fingers trembling over the keyboard.

Because how could she write love stories when she had let hers go?

Riya noticed.

"You're miserable," she said one afternoon, flopping onto Taarika's bed.

Taarika scoffed. "I am not miserable."

Riya raised an eyebrow. "You haven't written in weeks. You sigh dramatically at least twenty times a day. And your coffee intake is concerning even for you."

Taarika crossed her arms. "That proves nothing."

Riya smirked. "You miss him."

Taarika's chest tightened.

Of course she did.

But missing someone wasn't enough to bring them back.

Right?

....

Aarav's Unsent Message

Aarav stared at his phone, thumb hovering over Taarika's contact.

He had typed out a message five times. Deleted it five times.

Aarav: Hey, I— (Backspace. Too casual.)

Aarav: I miss you. (Too vulnerable.)

Aarav: Are you okay? (Too desperate.)

He sighed, rubbing his temple.

And then, instead of texting, he did the only thing he knew how to do.

He wrote.

A song.

Not for the label. Not for his audience.

For her.

18

A Love That Won't Let Go

The Song That Reached Her First

Taarika wasn't expecting it.

She had just opened Instagram when she saw it.....Aarav's new song, posted without a caption.

Her heart pounded as she clicked on it.

Then.....his voice.

"I left, but you never really left me."

"I sing, but every note still sounds like your name."

"Maybe love is the silence between the words..."

"Maybe love is what stays... even when we don't."

Taarika's breath caught.

Because this wasn't just a song.

This was him reaching for her.

This was Aarav telling her he was still waiting.

And suddenly, she couldn't do this anymore.

She couldn't keep pretending she was fine.

She needed to see him.

....

The Train to Mumbai

"Are you sure about this?" Riya asked as she helped Taarika pack a bag.

Taarika zipped up her suitcase, determination in her eyes.

"Yes."

She had spent too long running from what she wanted.

Now, she was ready to fight for it.

....

The Mumbai Reunion

Aarav was in his studio when he heard the knock.

He frowned, setting his guitar down. No one visited him here.

But when he opened the door......

His breath caught.

Taarika.

Standing there.

Looking at him like he was the song she had been trying to write all this time.

Neither of them spoke.

Then.......

She stepped forward.

Grabbed his face between her hands.

And whispered, "You're not the only one who's been waiting."

Then she kissed him.

And this time, she wasn't going anywhere.

19
Almost Forever

The Weight of Goodbye

Love wasn't supposed to feel like this.

Like a goodbye waiting to happen.

Like something slipping through her fingers no matter how tightly she tried to hold on.

Taarika had come to Mumbai thinking she could fix this. That she could finally be brave.

And for a while, it worked.

For a while, it was just them…..writing their story in late-night conversations and stolen kisses on Aarav's rooftop, where the city lights flickered beneath them like scattered stars.

But dreams didn't pause for love.

And reality had a way of reminding them that choosing each other meant losing something else.

Aarav had a contract. A career waiting to take off.

And Taarika?

Taarika had an offer from a publishing house in Delhi.

Her book....the one she had poured her soul into...was finally getting published.

And suddenly, they weren't just two people in love.

They were two people with dreams pulling them in different directions.

....

The Hardest Decision

They sat on Aarav's rooftop that night, wrapped in the silence of everything they weren't saying.

Aarav strummed his guitar absently, the melody soft, unfinished.

Taarika hugged her knees to her chest, staring at the horizon.

Finally, he spoke.

"So, Delhi?"

She swallowed hard. "Yeah."

Aarav nodded slowly. "That's amazing."

"It is."

A pause.

Then............

"Then why do you look like you're about to cry?"

Taarika blinked rapidly, biting her lip. "Because I don't know how to choose."

Aarav's fingers stilled on the strings.

"Taarika." He turned to face her fully. "I never want to be the reason you don't chase your dreams."

Tears welled in her eyes. "And I don't want to be the reason you don't chase yours."

He exhaled sharply, running a hand through his hair. "So what do we do?"

Taarika let out a shaky breath. "Maybe... we say goodbye before we start resenting each other for staying."

The words tasted like heartbreak.

Aarav stared at her, something breaking behind his eyes.

Then, he set his guitar down and reached for her hand.

His fingers were warm, steady.

His voice, when he spoke, was barely above a whisper.

"I love you."

Taarika's breath hitched.

She had waited so long to hear those words.

And now, when she finally had them, she had to let them go.

"I love you too," she whispered.

Then, before she could change her mind.....before she could beg him to ask her to stay......

She kissed him.

It was slow. Desperate. A last attempt to memorize the way he felt.

And when she finally pulled away, her heart shattered at the look in his eyes.

Because she knew.

This was their last kiss.

Aarav's voice was hoarse. "Stay."

Taarika closed her eyes. "I can't."

Then she turned and walked away.

And this time, he didn't stop her.

Because sometimes, love meant knowing when to let go.

20

If We're Meant to Be

The Aftermath of Goodbye

Taarika thought leaving would be easier if she didn't look back.

But she did.

She looked back at the airport. At her phone screen, where Aarav's contact sat untouched. At the empty seat beside her on the train to Delhi, where she imagined him sitting.

Everywhere she went, she looked for him.

But he wasn't there.

And that was the hardest part.

Because for the first time since she met him, she was learning what life felt like without Aarav.

And it hurt.

....

Aarav's Silence

Mumbai felt different without her.

Aarav tried to throw himself into his music, into the career he had dreamed of for years.

But every song he wrote sounded like her.

Every stage felt too big, too empty.

And his heart?

His heart wasn't in it.

He had let her go because he thought it was the right thing to do.

But what if letting go was the biggest mistake of his life?

....

The Song That Changed Everything

One night, when the emptiness became unbearable, Aarav did something reckless.

He picked up his guitar.

Pressed 'record.'

And sang.

"You left, but you never really left me."

"I let go, but I never really did."

"If love is written in the spaces between us,"

"Then maybe we were never really over."

He didn't think.

Didn't plan.

He just posted it.

And within hours, the internet exploded.

....

Taarika's Realization

Taarika was in the middle of a meeting at her publishing house when her phone started buzzing uncontrollably.

She frowned, pulling it out....

And then her heart stopped.

Aarav's new song was everywhere.

Trending on Twitter. Flooding her Instagram feed. Playing on repeat in every café.

And the title?

"If We're Meant to Be."

Her hands trembled as she clicked on the video.

And the second his voice filled the room, she knew.

She had to go back.

She had to find him.

Because if they were meant to be, she wasn't going to wait for fate to decide.

She was going to fight for him.

21

A Moment That Felt Like Fate

The Flight Back to Him

Taarika had never been one to believe in fate.

But as she sat on the flight back to Mumbai, heart racing with every passing second, she couldn't shake the feeling that this.......this moment, this decision.......was always meant to happen.

Her fingers gripped the armrest as the plane began its descent. She had spent months convincing herself that letting Aarav go had been the right choice.

And yet, here she was.

Running straight back to him.

Because love wasn't something you could just walk away from. Not when it felt like this.

Not when it felt inevitable.

....

The Rain-Soaked Reunion

It was raining when she reached the venue.

Aarav had just finished his performance. She could hear the last echoes of his song fading into the night, his voice lingering in the humid Mumbai air.

Her heart pounded.

She hadn't planned what to say. Hadn't even let herself think beyond finding him.

And then............

She saw him.

Standing near the backstage exit, head tilted toward the sky, rain dripping from his hair.

She froze.

Because suddenly, it wasn't just a reunion.

It was a memory.

The first time they had met in the rain. The first time she had heard him play.

The first time she had realized he was going to change her life.

Aarav turned as if he felt her presence.

His eyes widened.

"Taarika?"

She swallowed hard, stepping forward.

"I never stopped loving you."

Aarav's breath hitched.

And just like that, the space between them disappeared.

He pulled her close, his hands framing her face like he was afraid she would vanish.

Then, softly.....

"Neither did I."

And as their lips met, the rain fell harder.......

Washing away the distance.

Washing away the past.

Leaving nothing behind but them.

22

More Than Just a Picture

The Morning After the Storm

Taarika woke up to the sound of music.

For a moment, she thought she was still dreaming.

But when she blinked her eyes open, there he was.

Aarav. Sitting on the floor of his apartment, guitar resting on his lap, quietly strumming a melody that made her heart ache.

She watched him for a moment, taking in the way he looked so completely lost in the music.

Like this was his way of telling her everything he couldn't put into words.

She smiled. "Are you writing about me again?"

Aarav looked up, smirking. "I never stopped."

Taarika rolled her eyes but couldn't fight the warmth spreading through her chest.

She sat up, hugging her knees. "So… what happens now?"

Aarav set his guitar down, shifting so he was facing her.

"Now," he said, "we stop running."

She bit her lip. "And if it gets hard?"

Aarav smiled softly. "Then we fight for it."

And just like that……….

They weren't a question anymore.

They were an answer.

……….

Making It Official

That afternoon, Aarav did something unexpected.

He took Taarika's hand, pulled out his phone, and snapped a picture of them…her curled up beside him on the couch, his arm slung casually over her shoulders.

Then, without hesitation…..

He posted it.

Taarika's eyes widened. "Wait….Aarav"

Too late.

Within minutes, his followers flooded the comments.

@AaravSings: No more unwritten songs. No more unfinished stories.

Taarika groaned, burying her face in her hands. "You just made it public?"

Aarav chuckled, pressing a kiss to her temple. "Yeah. Because I don't want to hide you."

And maybe.....just maybe.....she didn't want to be hidden anymore either.

Facing the Past One Last Time

Taarika had never been the jealous type.

But when Aarav's phone buzzed later that night, and she saw the name on the screen...Mebi...her heart clenched.

Aarav noticed. "It's nothing."

But Taarika shook her head. "Answer it."

Aarav hesitated.

Then, finally, he picked up.

"Mebi." His voice was firm. "Why are you calling?"

There was a pause. Then.......

"I saw the picture," Mebi said. "So it's real, huh?"

Aarav's jaw tightened. "It's real."

Mebi sighed. "I just... I wanted to say I'm happy for you."

Taarika blinked in surprise.

She had expected something else. A challenge. A reminder of the past.

But not this.

Aarav nodded. "Thank you."

And just like that, the past was behind them.

This time, there were no doubts.

No unfinished endings.

Only the present.

And the promise of everything yet to come.

23

A Love That Feels Like Home

A New Beginning in an Old Place

Taarika never thought she'd find herself back in The Lantern Library, sitting at the same table where she had first met Aarav.

But this time, everything was different.

This time, she wasn't just watching him play his guitar....she was part of the story.

The space between them wasn't filled with hesitation or unspoken emotions anymore. It was filled with certainty.

Aarav glanced up from his guitar, smirking. "You're staring."

Taarika rolled her eyes. "I'm just trying to figure out how you still haven't finished that song."

Aarav chuckled, strumming a few chords. "Maybe I was waiting for the right ending."

She tilted her head. "And have you found it yet?"

Aarav met her gaze, something soft in his eyes.

"I think I just did."

Her heart flipped.

Because for the first time, she wasn't scared of where this was going.

She knew where it was going.

....

The Surprise That Changed Everything

Later that evening, Aarav had a surprise for her.

"Come with me," he said, grabbing her hand and leading her out of the library.

Taarika frowned. "Where are we going?"

Aarav just smiled. "Trust me."

Ten minutes later, they stood in front of a small, empty café space tucked into a quiet street of Manesar.

Taarika's eyes widened. "Aarav... what is this?"

He turned to her, eyes shining. "A dream."

Her breath hitched as realization sank in.

The wooden sign above the door read:

Chapters & Chords.

Her hands flew to her mouth. "You…"

"I want to build something with you, Taarika," Aarav said softly. "A place where music and stories come together. Where you can write and I can play, and people can walk in and feel something."

Tears burned at the corners of her eyes.

She had spent so long believing that love meant choosing between dreams.

But standing here, in front of the café that carried both their passions, she realized.....

Maybe love wasn't about choosing.

Maybe love was about creating something together.

And this?

This was their something.

24

A Love That Can't Be Shaken

The First Fight That Mattered

The next few weeks were filled with laughter, long nights of planning, and endless cups of coffee as they worked on bringing Chapters & Chords to life.

But love, no matter how deep, wasn't without its challenges.

And one night, the first crack appeared.

It started as a small disagreement....Taarika wanted the café to have more of a bookshop feel, while Aarav envisioned it as a live music venue first.

But somewhere along the way, frustration crept in.

"You don't listen," Taarika snapped, crossing her arms. "You make decisions without asking me."

Aarav ran a hand through his hair. "Because if we overthink every little thing, this place will never open."

Taarika's chest tightened. "This isn't just your dream, Aarav. It's ours."

His expression softened. "I know that."

Silence.

Then, quietly........

"I'm just scared."

Taarika frowned. "Of what?"

Aarav exhaled, looking away. "That this... us... this café... is too good to be real. That something will go wrong."

Her heart clenched.

She stepped forward, reaching for his hand. "Then we fight for it."

Aarav looked at her, his grip tightening around hers.

And just like that, the tension melted away.

Because love wasn't just about passion or romance.

Love was about choosing each other even when it was hard.

And they were choosing each other.

....

The Grand Opening

The day Chapters & Chords opened, the café was filled with the people who had been part of their story from the very beginning.

Riya.

Ishaan.

Even Aarav's old music mentor, who had always believed in his talent.

As the evening sun dipped below the horizon, Aarav stepped onto the small café stage, his guitar slung over his shoulder.

He glanced at Taarika, who stood by the bookshelf, watching him with a soft smile.

And then......he sang.

"Some love stories are written in ink,"

"Some in the spaces between the words."

"Ours was written in the melodies,"

"In every note, in every chord."

Taarika's throat tightened.

Because this was their story.

This was their forever.

And as Aarav reached for her hand, pulling her onto the stage beside him, she realized........

She wasn't just part of his story.

She was his favorite song.

25
Closing the Last Page

———❤———

A Quiet Moment Before Forever

The café was finally open.

The shelves were lined with books, the scent of coffee mixed with the soft hum of music, and the small stage in the corner carried the promise of endless melodies waiting to be played.

Chapters & Chords wasn't just a café.

It was them.

Their love, their story, their dreams woven into every inch of the place.

But as beautiful as the present was, there was still a page from the past that needed to be closed.

And it came in the form of an unexpected message.

....

Aarav's Final Goodbye to Mebi

Taarika was rearranging the books near the counter when she noticed Aarav staring at his phone, jaw tight, brows furrowed.

"What's wrong?" she asked, setting down a book.

Aarav hesitated, then turned the screen toward her.

A message.

Mebi: Can we talk? One last time?

Taarika's heart clenched.

She knew this moment would come eventually.

Aarav's past was something she had made peace with. But that didn't mean seeing Mebi's name didn't sting just a little.

She swallowed. "Are you going to meet her?"

Aarav exhaled, setting his phone down. "Only if you're okay with it."

Taarika studied his face. There was no hesitation in his voice, no hidden emotion.

This wasn't a meeting to rekindle old feelings.

This was a meeting to end them once and for all.

So she nodded. "Go."

Aarav gave her a grateful smile, squeezing her hand before walking out.

And suddenly, she wasn't afraid.

Because she knew...his heart wasn't with Mebi anymore.

It was with her.

....

The Last Conversation

Aarav met Mebi in the Mall on the other side of town.

She looked different......older, more mature, but there was still that same knowing smile on her lips when she saw him.

"So," Mebi sighed, stirring her coke, "you finally got the happy ending."

Aarav tilted his head. "Didn't we both?"

Mebi chuckled. "I suppose we did." She took a deep breath. "I just wanted to say... I'm sorry."

Aarav frowned. "For what?"

"For hurting you. For making you believe that love wasn't worth fighting for."

Aarav was quiet for a moment before he spoke. "I needed to go through that to understand what love really is."

Mebi smiled, but this time, it was genuine. "And what is it?"

Aarav's lips twitched. "Love is when you don't have to question if the other person will stay."

Mebi exhaled, nodding. "She's lucky."

Aarav shook his head. "I'm the lucky one."

And just like that, the past finally felt like the past.

When Aarav walked out of the Mall, he felt lighter.

And as he made his way back to Chapters & Chords, he realized........

This was the first time in years that his heart felt completely, undeniably free.

Because he wasn't holding on to anything anymore.

Except Taarika.

26
Love in the Little Things

A Love That Felt Like Home

Aarav walked into the café just as Taarika was finishing up for the day.

She turned, and the second their eyes met, she knew.

"It's over?" she asked softly.

Aarav nodded.

And then, without another word, he pulled her into his arms, holding her tightly against his chest.

Taarika melted into him, her fingers clutching the back of his shirt, breathing in the familiar scent of coffee and music and home.

Because that's what he was.

Her home.

"Did you get the closure you needed?" she whispered.

Aarav pulled back just enough to cup her face, his thumb brushing against her cheek.

"I didn't need closure, Taarika," he murmured. "I just needed to come back to you."

Her heart swelled.

And suddenly, she realized........

This was it.

This was the kind of love she had always written about but never believed she would have.

The kind that wasn't just grand gestures and poetic words.

The kind that existed in the quiet moments.

In the way he made her coffee exactly how she liked it.

In the way he always pulled her closer in his sleep.

In the way he looked at her like she was the most important thing in the world.

And maybe she was.

Maybe they were.

....

The First Night of Forever

Later that night, as they sat on the floor of the café, surrounded by books and guitars and the warmth of something real, Aarav reached for his guitar.

Taarika arched a brow. "Another song?"

Aarav smirked. "A special one."

He started playing, his voice soft, the melody familiar.

"Some love stories end before they begin."

"Some get lost in the spaces between."

"But ours was written in ink that won't fade,"

"A story that no ending can break."

Taarika's throat tightened. "Aarav…"

He set the guitar down and turned to her, pulling a small velvet box from his pocket.

Her heart stopped.

Aarav took a deep breath, eyes locked onto hers.

"Taarika Sharma," he said, voice steady, certain. "You are my favorite story. The only song I want to keep writing. And I don't want to spend another second of my life without you."

He opened the box, revealing a simple but beautiful ring.

"Will you marry me?"

Taarika's hands flew to her mouth, tears spilling before she could even speak.

And in that moment, she didn't feel fear.

She didn't feel doubt.

She only felt love.

"Yes," she whispered.

Aarav let out a shaky laugh before slipping the ring onto her finger.

And then, as he kissed her...slow, deep, forever....she knew.

This wasn't just a love story.

This was their forever

27
Closing the Chapter on the Past

The sunlight streamed through the windows of Chapters & Chords, casting a golden glow over the wooden shelves and the small stage where Aarav had once poured his heart into music.

Taarika stood behind the counter, staring at the ring on her finger, still unable to believe that this wasn't just a dream.

She traced the delicate band with her thumb, a soft smile playing on her lips.

She was engaged.

To him.

To the boy who had walked into The Lantern Library with a guitar and a storm behind his eyes.

To the boy who had turned her words into music.

To the boy who had made her believe in forevers.

And now?

He was hers.

Forever.

The thought sent a shiver down her spine, one of excitement, of disbelief, of pure happiness.

And just as she was getting lost in her thoughts, she felt a pair of arms wrap around her from behind.

"Still staring at the ring?" Aarav's voice was warm, teasing.

Taarika laughed, leaning into his embrace. "It's still surreal."

Aarav rested his chin on her shoulder, his lips brushing her cheek. "Well, you better get used to it, fiancée."

The word sent a thrill through her.

Fiancée.

She turned in his arms, looping her hands around his neck. "You're insufferable."

Aarav grinned. "And yet, you agreed to marry me."

She rolled her eyes but couldn't fight the smile that tugged at her lips.

Because he was right.

She had said yes.

And she would say yes a thousand times more.

....

A Final Goodbye to the Past

A week after their engagement, Aarav did something unexpected.

He called Mebi.

Not because he had doubts. Not because there were lingering feelings.

But because he wanted to close the past completely.

Taarika sat beside him on the café couch, watching as he put the call on speaker.

The phone rang twice before Mebi answered.

"Aarav?"

"Hey," he said, his voice calm, steady. "I wanted to talk."

There was a pause. Then........

"I saw the engagement news," Mebi said. "Congratulations."

Taarika glanced at Aarav, waiting for his response.

Aarav nodded, though Mebi couldn't see it. "Thank you. And I just... I wanted to say that I hope you're happy too."

Mebi exhaled softly. "I am."

Another silence.

Then Mebi added, "You were right, you know. About love."

Aarav frowned. "What do you mean?"

"You once told me that real love doesn't make you question if someone will stay," she said. "I didn't understand it then. But now I do."

Aarav exchanged a glance with Taarika, squeezing her hand.

"Take care, Mebi," he said softly.

"You too," she replied.

And just like that, the past was no longer something that haunted him.

Because when he hung up, he didn't feel regret.

He felt free.

And when he turned to Taarika, he realized....

She was the only future he wanted.

28
The Crossroads of Love

A Dream That Came True...But at a Cost

The chapters and chords was thriving.

The dream they had built together was now real...filled with books, music, laughter, and the warmth of something that felt like home.

But with success came new challenges.

And one of them arrived in the form of two unexpected emails.

The first?

Taarika's publisher wanted her to move to Delhi full-time.

The second?

Aarav had been offered an international music tour.

And suddenly, they were back at the crossroads they thought they had left behind.

Back to choosing between love and their dreams.

....

The Unspoken Tension

For days, neither of them talked about it.

Taarika buried herself in work at the café, pretending she wasn't rereading the email over and over again.

Aarav played his music, pretending he wasn't imagining the crowds in different cities.

But the silence wasn't fooling either of them.

Finally, one evening, Aarav broke it.

"Are you going to take it?" he asked, leaning against the counter as she stacked books.

Taarika froze, her fingers tightening around the book in her hands.

She took a slow breath. "Are you?"

Aarav didn't answer right away. Instead, he set his guitar down and walked over to her.

"Taarika," he murmured, tilting her chin up so she had to meet his gaze. "We promised not to run from each other again."

Taarika swallowed. "But what if this time... we have to?"

Aarav's jaw tightened. "Are you saying we should let go?"

Her heart clenched. "No."

He exhaled, relief flickering in his eyes. "Then what are we saying?"

She shook her head, voice breaking. "I don't know."

Because how do you choose between the love of your life and the dreams you spent your whole life chasing?

....

A Night of Answers

That night, they didn't sleep.

They sat on the café floor, surrounded by books and guitars, their fingers entwined.

Talking.

Dreaming.

Searching for answers in the spaces between them.

And then, as the clock struck 3 AM, Aarav exhaled and finally said it.

"I don't think we have to choose."

Taarika frowned. "What do you mean?"

Aarav squeezed her hand. "What if we make this work? Long distance, late-night calls, visiting whenever we can.

What if we don't have to give up either?"

Taarika's breath hitched.

She had always thought love meant being in the same place, choosing one over the other.

But what if love meant fighting, even from a distance?

Slowly, a smile tugged at her lips.

"Are you sure?" she whispered.

Aarav smiled, pressing his forehead against hers. "I've never been more sure of anything in my life."

And just like that, they weren't at a crossroads anymore.

They were walking forward....together.

....

A Love That Didn't Need an Ending

The night before Taarika left for Delhi and Aarav left for his tour, they stood outside the café, fingers intertwined.

Taarika bit her lip. "You know, in every love story I've written, distance ruins things."

Aarav smirked. "Then I guess we'll just have to prove you wrong."

She chuckled. "You're insufferable."

He leaned in, brushing his lips against hers. "And yet, you're still marrying me."

She smiled against his lips. "Yeah. I am."

And in that moment, under the glow of their café sign, under the sky that had witnessed their love from the beginning.

29
Love in the Spaces Between

The First Night Apart

Distance wasn't just measured in miles.

It was in the absence of his laughter in the café, in the missing warmth of his touch, in the silence that followed when she reached for her phone and realized he wasn't just a few streets away anymore.

Taarika lay in bed that night, staring at the ceiling, the soft hum of the city outside her window.

She should have been excited.

Her book was being published. Her dream of becoming an author was finally coming true.

But all she could think about was him.

Somewhere across the country, Aarav was in another city, standing in front of a crowd, playing the songs that once belonged only to her.

And she wondered.....was he thinking about her too?

Her phone buzzed.

She grabbed it instantly.

Aarav: Can't sleep. You?

A smile ghosted across her lips.

Taarika: Same.

A pause. Then.....

Aarav: You could just admit you miss me, Sharma.

She rolled her eyes, typing quickly.

Taarika: You're insufferable.

Aarav: And yet, you're still in love with me.

Her fingers hesitated over the keyboard.

Then....

Taarika: Yeah. I am.

Aarav's reply was instant.

Aarav: Good. Because I love you too.

And just like that, the distance didn't feel so big anymore.

....

The Little Things That Kept Them Together

Distance wasn't easy.

There were missed calls and time zone differences, bad Wi-Fi connections and nights that felt lonelier than they should have.

But they made it work.

Because love wasn't just in the big gestures. It was in the little things.

It was in the way Aarav would send her voice notes of new melodies he was working on, waiting for her to tell him what they reminded her of.

It was in the way Taarika would text him random quotes from her book, just to hear his opinion.

It was in the surprise deliveries....Aarav sending her her favorite coffee on days she was drowning in deadlines, Taarika having a handwritten letter delivered to him before his first international show.

It was in the spaces between the calls, in the unspoken understanding that no matter how far they were.....

They were still each other's home.

....

Aarav's Biggest Stage Yet

The night of Aarav's biggest concert, Taarika sat in her apartment, watching the live stream.

Thousands of people filled the stadium, chanting his name. He looked different, standing on that massive stage, lights flashing around him.

But the second he stepped up to the microphone, his voice smooth and steady, she saw her Aarav.

And when he smiled slightly before speaking, she knew.......

He was about to do something reckless.

"This next song," Aarav said, voice echoing through the stadium, "isn't just a song."

He paused.

"It's a letter. To the girl who turned my melodies into something more. To the one who made me believe that love isn't about being in the same place....it's about choosing someone, no matter the distance."

Taarika's breath hitched.

Then, he played.

"Some love is fireworks, burning bright and fast,"

"Some love is quiet, the kind that lasts."

"And even if the world pulls us apart,"

"I'll find my way back to where you are."

Taarika wiped at her cheeks, laughing through her tears.

Because of course he had written her a song.

And as his voice filled the stadium, she knew.....

No matter where he went, his heart would always belong to her.

30
The Moment That Felt Like Home

Coming Back to Where It All Began

Two months.

That's how long they had been apart.

Two months of video calls, voice notes, stolen moments through screens.

But nothing compared to this.

To finally standing in front of him again.

The second Taarika stepped off the train in Manesar, her heart pounded so hard she thought it might burst.

And then....

She saw him.

Standing at the edge of the platform, hands shoved into his pockets, eyes searching for her.

The second his gaze met hers, the world tilted.

And suddenly, nothing else mattered.

She didn't think. Didn't hesitate.

She ran.

Straight into his arms.

Aarav caught her, laughing as she buried her face in his neck.

"I missed you," she whispered, her voice breaking.

Aarav tightened his grip around her. "Not as much as I missed you."

She pulled back slightly, just enough to look at him.

"You're real," she murmured, tracing her fingers over his face, as if convincing herself he was actually standing in front of her.

Aarav chuckled. "I hope so. Otherwise, this is a really elaborate dream."

Taarika rolled her eyes, but before she could say anything, he cupped her face and kissed her.

Soft. Slow.

A reunion.

A promise.

A reminder that no matter where they went, they would always find their way back to each other.

....

The Surprise That Stole Her Breath

Later that evening, as they sat on the rooftop of Chapters & Chords, Aarav turned to her, a mischievous glint in his eyes.

"I have something for you," he said.

Taarika frowned. "Aarav, you don't have to"

But he was already reaching into his pocket.

And when he pulled out a key, her breath hitched.

"What is this?" she whispered.

Aarav smiled. "A key to our home."

Her heart stopped.

"Our... home?"

Aarav nodded. "I got an apartment here. Close to the café. So that no matter where we go, no matter what happens...we always have a place to come back to."

Taarika's hands trembled as she took the key from him, staring at it like it held the entire universe.

Because it did.

It held love.

It held forever.

And when she looked up at him, her eyes filled with everything she never had to say out loud.

Because he already knew.

She launched herself at him, wrapping her arms around his neck, pressing kisses to his jaw, his cheeks, his lips.

Aarav laughed, holding her close.

"Does this mean you like it?" he teased.

Taarika sniffled, swatting his arm. "You idiot. I love it."

Aarav grinned. "Then let's go home."

And just like that....

They weren't just a love story anymore.

They were a home.

A love that didn't just survive distance....

A love that always found its way back.

31
The Dream They Built Together

The One-Year Anniversary of Chapters & Chords

One year.

That's how long it had been since they had turned an empty space into a home for dreamers.

And now, on its first anniversary, the café was more than just a place.

It was a love story of its own.

The shelves were lined with books that had been read and loved. The walls held Polaroids of their journey...pictures of the café's opening night, candid shots of Aarav playing on the small stage, stolen moments of Taarika writing in the corner.

And tonight, the café was packed.

Friends. Family. Strangers who had become regulars.

They had all gathered for the special night of music and stories.

Aarav stood on stage, adjusting his guitar.

When he looked up, his eyes went straight to her.

Taarika, standing near the counter, watching him with the same look she always had...like he was the only thing in the world that mattered.

Aarav smiled.

And then, he spoke into the mic.

"I wasn't always the kind of guy who believed in fate," he admitted. "I used to think love was just something people wrote about. Something that faded. But then, I met a girl who wrote between the lines, and suddenly, I realized....the best love stories aren't just written. They're lived."

The crowd cheered, but Taarika's breath caught.

Because she knew....this song was for her.

And as Aarav played, the lyrics told their story.

"She was ink, I was chords, two stories yet to meet."

"She wrote in silence, I played in melody."

"And somehow in between the words and the sound,"

"We found love, and we let it stay."

Taarika wiped at her cheeks, laughing through her tears.

Because this wasn't just a song.

It was their beginning, their middle, and their forever.

....

A Proposal That Took Her Breath Away (Again)

After the show, as the last guests trickled out, Aarav pulled Taarika aside.

"I have something for you," he said.

Taarika frowned. "Aarav, you've already given me enough surprises tonight."

Aarav smirked. "Trust me, you'll like this one."

He pulled out a notebook, slightly worn, filled with his handwriting.

Taarika blinked. "What is this?"

Aarav smiled. "Your book."

Her breath hitched. "What?"

Aarav rubbed the back of his neck. "I know you've been struggling with the ending. So... I thought I'd help."

She flipped through the pages, her chest tightening as she read.

It was their story.

From the first time they met to the moment she had run back to him. Every fight, every song, every word left unsaid...now written down in ink.

Taarika clutched the notebook to her chest, her heart overflowing.

"Aarav..."

He stepped closer, pressing a kiss to her forehead.

"Marry me again," he whispered. "Not just in words, not just in plans. But every day, in the little moments, in the spaces between us."

Taarika let out a breathless laugh, shaking her head. "You're ridiculous."

Aarav grinned. "Is that a yes?"

She threw her arms around his neck. "It's a forever."

32
Love Between the Lines

The Last Chapter That Never Ends

Some stories had endings.

Theirs didn't.

Because love...real love...wasn't just in the grand gestures or the big moments.

It was in the late-night writing sessions, where Taarika read him the words she could never say aloud.

It was in the soft kisses behind the café counter, in the way Aarav still played her love songs even when she rolled her eyes.

It was in the forever they were building...one note, one word, one moment at a time.

And as Taarika sat at Chapters & Chords, typing the final lines of her book, she realized.....

She wasn't just writing a love story anymore.

She was living it.

Because this?

This was love between the lines.

And it was only just beginning.

....

In the morning, Taarika stretched lazily, the scent of coffee filling the air as she blinked her eyes open.

Aarav was standing by the kitchen counter, barefoot, his hair messy from sleep, humming a tune as he poured coffee into two mugs.

Aarav turned, catching her watching him. He smirked. "Morning, Writer Girl."

Taarika rolled her eyes but smiled as she sat up. "Morning, Rockstar."

He walked over, handing her the coffee before sitting beside her on the couch.

"So," he said, nudging her shoulder, "how does it feel? Living with me?"

Taarika smirked, pretending to think. "Messy. Loud. A little dramatic."

Aarav gasped. "Dramatic? Me?"

She laughed, taking a sip of coffee. "But..." She hesitated.

Aarav watched her. "But?"

She met his gaze, something vulnerable in her eyes. "But it feels like home."

Aarav's smirk softened, his fingers brushing against hers. "Good. Because I don't want you anywhere else."

The moment stretched between them...warm, real, right.

And then....

A loud knock interrupted them.

Aarav frowned. "Who the hell is here this early?"

Taarika shrugged. "Did you order food?"

Aarav shook his head, standing up and opening the door.

And immediately froze.

Because standing there, with matching amused expressions, were his parents.

....

Aarav's Parents & Their Unexpected Visit

"Aarav," his mother, Meera, said with a knowing smile. "Are you going to invite us in, or should we just assume we're not welcome?"

Aarav blinked. "Mom? Dad?"

His father, Arvind, chuckled. "Surprised?"

Aarav rubbed the back of his neck. "Uh... yeah."

Taarika, still sitting on the couch, felt her heartbeat pick up. She had met Aarav's parents once before, but back then, they weren't living together.

Now?

Now, his mother was eyeing the cozy little apartment, her gaze landing on Taarika, who was still in her oversized T-shirt and Aarav's hoodie.

Oh.

Oh no.

Aarav finally stepped aside, letting them in. "Not that I don't love seeing you guys, but what are you doing here?"

Meera smiled. "We had a wedding to attend in Mumbai, so we thought we'd surprise you." She paused, eyes twinkling. "Looks like we weren't the only ones with surprises."

Taarika resisted the urge to bury herself under the couch.

Aarav sighed, running a hand through his hair. "Mom, Dad, you remember Taarika?"

Arvind nodded, smiling warmly. "Of course. The writer."

Taarika quickly stood, offering a polite smile. "Hello, Uncle. Aunty."

Meera looked between them, then at the apartment, then back at them. "So… are you two living together?"

Aarav hesitated for half a second before saying, "Yeah. We are."

Taarika choked on air.

Couldn't he have eased into that instead of just dropping the bomb?

Meera's eyes sparkled with something unreadable. "I see."

Aarav, sensing the tension, quickly added, "Mom, it's not"

Meera waved him off. "Oh, relax. I'm not judging. I'm just… observing."

Which, honestly, was worse.

Arvind sat down, looking around. "Nice place. Cozy." He smirked at Aarav. "Bet Taarika keeps it organized."

Taarika chuckled nervously. "I try."

Aarav threw his father a betrayed look. "I keep it organized."

Meera snorted. "Sweetheart, you once lost your own shoes in your bedroom. You are not the organized one."

Taarika laughed.

Aarav groaned. "Okay, can we not team up against me?"

His father patted his shoulder. "No promises, son."

33
The Unspoken Approval

As the evening went on, the initial awkwardness faded.

Taarika cooked while Aarav's mother helped, exchanging stories about Aarav's childhood...embarrassing ones, of course.

"You know," Meera said as they chopped vegetables, "Aarav once tried to write a love letter to a girl in tenth grade."

Taarika's eyes widened. "Oh?"

Aarav groaned from across the room. "Mom, no."

Meera ignored him. "He was too nervous to give it to her, so he left it in her book."

Taarika smirked. "And?"

Meera giggled. "He put it in the wrong book. A math book. The girl never found it."

Taarika burst out laughing. "Oh my God."

Aarav covered his face. "This is trauma, not entertainment."

Meera winked at Taarika. "And now he writes songs instead of love letters. Much safer."

Taarika smiled. "Well, I like his songs."

Meera studied her for a moment, something soft in her gaze.

And then, she said, "You love him, don't you?"

Taarika's breath hitched.

She hadn't said it out loud yet. Not even to Aarav.

But Meera saw it. Felt it.

Taarika exhaled. And then, quietly....

"I do."

Meera nodded, pleased. "Good."

Taarika blinked. "Good?"

Meera smiled. "Because he loves you, too."

Her heart skipped a beat.

And in that moment, she realized....

She didn't need to be afraid anymore.

....

Later That Night

After his parents left, Taarika stood on the balcony, the Mumbai skyline stretching endlessly before her.

Aarav walked up behind her, wrapping his arms around her waist. "You survived my mother."

Taarika laughed. "Barely."

Aarav kissed the side of her head. "She likes you."

Taarika turned in his arms, looking up at him. "I like her, too."

Aarav smirked. "You told her you love me."

Taarika's stomach flipped. "She told you?"

Aarav grinned. "Of course. She was waiting for me to gloat."

Taarika groaned. "God, I'm never going to win against her, am I?"

Aarav chuckled. "Nope."

She sighed dramatically. "Great."

Aarav cupped her face, his gaze softening. "But... you do, don't you?"

Taarika's heart pounded.

And for once, she didn't let fear win.

She smiled.

And whispered......

"I do."

Aarav grinned. "Say it again."

She rolled her eyes but laughed. "I love you, Aarav."

And then, he kissed her.

Slow, deep, like he was memorizing the moment.

Like this....them....was home.

And for the first time, she believed it.

34
The Proposal Neither of Them Expected

Aarav and Taarika had built a life together....one filled with lazy mornings, late-night songwriting sessions, and stolen kisses between coffee breaks. They had fallen into a rhythm that felt effortless, like they had been doing this forever.

But as much as they felt like husband and wife, there was one thing they hadn't done...made it official.

And Aarav's parents? They weren't going to let that slide.

....

The Unexpected Conversation

It started casually enough.

Meera and Arvind had invited them for dinner at their Mumbai hotel before heading back to Manesar.

Taarika should have sensed something was off when Aarav's mother insisted on ordering all of their favorite dishes, as if softening them up for something.

Aarav, oblivious, was focused on his plate, happily munching on butter naan. "Mom, I don't know what this dinner is about, but if you keep feeding me like this, I won't complain."

Meera smirked. "Oh, don't worry, beta. You'll know soon enough."

Arvind cleared his throat, setting down his fork. "So… how long have you two been living together now?"

Taarika stiffened, suddenly hyper-aware of how much this sounded like an interrogation.

Aarav, still chewing, shrugged. "Six months."

Meera raised an eyebrow. "Six months."

Aarav nodded, clearly missing the sharp parental energy radiating from across the table.

Arvind leaned back in his chair. "And do you two have… plans?"

Taarika blinked. "Plans?"

Meera smiled sweetly. Too sweetly. "Yes, dear. You know, the proper kind of plans."

Taarika coughed, nearly choking on her drink.

Aarav frowned, finally catching on. "Wait... are you two" His eyes widened. "Are you trying to say we should get married?"

Meera sighed dramatically. "Finally, he understands."

Aarav looked between them, dumbfounded. "Mom, Dad, we're fine. We don't need"

"Oh no," Meera interrupted, shaking her head. "You need. You're already living together like a married couple, so why not be one?"

Taarika felt her face heat up. "Aunty, I..."

Meera turned to her. "Tell me, Taarika, when you imagine your future, does it have Aarav in it?"

Taarika opened her mouth. Closed it. Because the answer was obvious.

Aarav was her future.

But marriage? She hadn't even thought about it.

Meera sighed knowingly. "You love him."

Taarika swallowed. "Yes."

Meera smiled. "And he loves you."

Aarav frowned. "Obviously."

Meera's eyes twinkled. "Then what's the problem?"

Silence.

Taarika and Aarav exchanged a look.

And suddenly, neither of them had an answer.

....

Aarav's Overreaction (That Wasn't Really an Overreaction)

The ride home was quiet.

Too quiet.

Taarika stole a glance at Aarav, who was gripping the steering wheel tighter than necessary.

She sighed. "Okay, say something."

Aarav exhaled sharply. "I just... I wasn't expecting that."

Taarika bit her lip. "Me neither."

Aarav tapped his fingers against the wheel. "I mean, it's not like I don't want to marry you."

Her heart skipped a beat.

He glanced at her. "I do."

She swallowed. "You do?"

Aarav scoffed. "Taarika. I've written you a hundred love songs. If that doesn't scream husband material, I don't know what does."

Taarika laughed softly. "You're ridiculous."

Aarav grinned. "And you love it."

She did.

But marriage? That was an entirely different kind of forever.

Aarav sighed. "Look, we don't have to do this just because our parents want us to." He looked at her, his voice softer now. "But if we do... it should be because we want to."

Taarika nodded. "Yeah. No pressure. No rush."

Aarav smirked. "Good. Because if I ever propose, it'll be epic."

Taarika rolled her eyes. "I swear, if there are fireworks involved"

Aarav wiggled his eyebrows. "Noted."

She groaned. "I hate you."

He chuckled. "That's unfortunate, considering you're going to marry me one day."

Taarika shoved him playfully. But deep down, her heart whispered something she wasn't ready to admit yet....

Maybe she actually wanted that too.

....

Aarav's Drunken Confession (Because Of Course He Had One)

Two nights later, Aarav came home tipsy after a "totally casual, not at all important band meeting."

Taarika, already in her pajamas, opened the door with a raised eyebrow. "You reek of whiskey."

Aarav grinned lazily. "That's 'cause I had whiskey."

She rolled her eyes, dragging him inside. "Wow, genius."

He flopped onto the couch, rubbing his face. "Taarika."

She sighed, grabbing water for him. "Yes?"

He blinked at her. "We should get married."

She froze.

"What?"

Aarav smiled sleepily. "You heard me."

Taarika's heart pounded. "Aarav. You're drunk."

He pointed a lazy finger at her. "No, no. I'm emotionally enlightened."

She fought a smile. "Oh really?"

Aarav nodded sagely. "And my emotional enlightenment says... I wanna marry you."

Taarika exhaled, setting the water down. "We are not doing this conversation while you're drunk."

Aarav groaned, running a hand through his hair. "Fine. But just so you know, sober-me thinks the same thing."

Her breath caught.

Because he meant it.

Even drunk, he meant every word.

She sighed, kneeling beside him. "Get some sleep, Rockstar."

Aarav grabbed her hand, squeezing it gently. "M'kay. But don't forget what I said."

Taarika smiled softly. "I won't."

But what Aarav didn't know was that she was already thinking about it too.

And maybe, just maybe—

She wanted to say yes.

35
A Proposal That Broke Us

Aarav always said that when he proposed, it would be epic.

And he wasn't lying.

The night he asked Taarika to marry him, it wasn't just between them.

It was in front of the whole world.

....

The Proposal That Went Viral

Taarika had been working late at Chapters & Chords, finalizing the new café menu, when her phone buzzed relentlessly.

Messages. Calls. Notifications.

Riya: Oh my god, have you seen YouTube?

Ananya (her cousin): TAARIKA. CHECK AARAV'S CHANNEL. NOW.

Unknown number: You're so lucky! This is every girl's dream!

Her heart pounded.

What did Aarav do?

With trembling fingers, she opened YouTube.

And there it was.....trending at #1.

"For My Writer Girl .... A Forever Song | Aarav Kapoor"

Her stomach flipped.

She clicked the video.

And then.......

There he was.

Aarav, sitting on their café stage, bathed in golden light, a guitar in his lap.

His voice was softer than she had ever heard, raw with emotion.

"She walked into my world with ink-stained hands,"

"Turned my silence into songs that finally made sense."

"And now I stand here, no fear, no doubt,"

"Because if love is a story, she's the one I want to write about."

Taarika's hands flew to her mouth.

The crowd in the video gasped as Aarav set down his guitar.

Then......

He pulled out a small velvet box.

"Taarika," he said, looking straight into the camera, as if he knew she was watching. "I don't want to wait another day. Marry me."

The café erupted into cheers.

The internet exploded.

And Taarika's heart...

Stopped.

Because while the world was celebrating, her world was about to fall apart.

....

The Call That Changed Everything

Before she could even process the video, her phone rang.

It was her mother.

Her stomach twisted.

She answered. "Maa, I...."

"Get home. Now."

Taarika froze. "What?"

"Now, Taarika!"

And just like that, she knew.....

Her family had seen it.

And they were furious.

....

House Arrested

She barely made it past the front door before her father slammed it shut behind her.

Her mother stood there, arms crossed, fury blazing in her eyes.

Her uncle was there too. And her aunt. And—

Taarika's breath caught.

Her cousin, Dev.

The boy her family had always wanted her to marry.

She turned to her father. "What is going on?"

Her mother threw the phone onto the table. The video was still playing.

"Marry me, Taarika."

Her father's voice was cold. "Tell me that this is a joke."

Taarika's hands trembled. "It's not."

Her uncle scoffed. "You've embarrassed this family."

Taarika's throat tightened. "I love him."

Her father's face darkened. "Enough."

Taarika's pulse pounded. "Papa, please"

"Enough!" he roared. "You have brought shame to us!"

Her mother grabbed her wrist. "You will never see him again."

Taarika's blood turned to ice.

She struggled. "You can't....."

Her father turned to her uncle. "Call the pandit. Arrange the wedding with Dev."

Taarika's world collapsed.

"No," she whispered.

Her mother's grip tightened. "Yes."

And just like that....

She was trapped.

....

Aarav's Panic

Meanwhile, Aarav was waiting.

Waiting for her to call. Waiting for her to show up.

But hours passed.

And then.......

His phone buzzed.

Unknown Number: She's gone.

Aarav frowned. "Who is this?"

Unknown Number: Her family took her. They won't let her out. They're forcing her to marry someone else.

Aarav's heart stopped.

No.

No, this wasn't happening.

He grabbed his keys and ran.

Because there was no way in hell he was losing her now.

....

Taarika's Shattered Heart

Locked in her room, Taarika stared at the walls, her chest aching.

Her phone was gone. The windows were barred.

And tomorrow.....

Tomorrow, she was supposed to become someone else's wife.

A tear slipped down her cheek.

Aarav...

Would he come for her?

Would he fight for her?

Or was this how their story ended?

She closed her eyes.

Prayed for a miracle.

And somewhere, across the city....

Aarav was already on his way.

36
The Fight for Forever

Taarika had never felt so helpless.

She sat on the cold floor of her childhood bedroom, the walls that once held her dreams now closing in like a prison.

Her wedding was tomorrow.

To a man she didn't love.

To a life she didn't choose.

And Aarav?

She didn't even know if he was coming.

Her mother had taken her phone. The windows were locked. Her father had posted relatives outside her door.

There was no escape.

Unless...

Unless she made one.

Her heart pounded.

She wouldn't let them write her ending.

Not when she had already chosen who she belonged to.

....

Meanwhile, Aarav Was Losing His Mind

He had been calling, texting, searching for her all night.

But there was nothing.

No response. No clue.

Only silence.

And that scared him more than anything.

Then......

His phone buzzed.

Riya: I found out where they're keeping her.

Aarav's pulse exploded.

"Where?!"

Riya: Her uncle's farmhouse. Guarded. No phone. They're marrying her off tomorrow morning.

Aarav felt rage rise in his chest.

"Not happening."

Riya: Aarav. This is dangerous.

Aarav's hands clenched around the steering wheel.

"So am I."

And then.......

He drove.

Because there was no way in hell he was losing her now.

....

The Wedding That Wasn't Meant to Be

The morning arrived too fast.

Taarika was dressed in bridal red, the weight of gold jewelry pressing against her skin.

She felt nothing.

Her mother fussed over her hair. Her father stood outside, greeting guests.

Dev, her so-called groom, waited at the mandap with a smirk.....because he knew she had no choice.

Taarika's heart pounded.

She had to get out.

She had to.....

BANG.

The doors flew open.

Gasps echoed through the hall.

And there.....drenched in sweat, eyes blazing with fury—stood Aarav.

Her world stopped.

....

The Fight That Changed Everything

Silence.

Then....

Her father's roar.

"GET HIM OUT!"

Relatives rushed forward. Hands grabbed Aarav's collar.

But he didn't care.

His eyes locked onto hers.

"Taarika."

Her breath hitched.

She ran.

Not toward her parents. Not toward safety.

Toward him.

Gasps filled the air as she threw herself into Aarav's arms.

Her mother shouted. Her father turned red.

Dev? Livid.

"Taarika, get back here!" her father yelled.

But she held onto Aarav tighter.

"No."

The word echoed.

Her father froze.

Her mother's eyes widened.

Because this time, she wasn't backing down.

Taarika turned, voice shaking.

"I love him. And I'm leaving."

Her father's face twisted in anger. "You think we'll let you go?"

Aarav stepped forward, voice low, dangerous.

"Try and stop us."

A tense silence.

Then......

Dev grabbed Aarav's arm. "You don't deserve her."

Aarav smiled darkly. "And you think you do?"

Then, in one swift punch, Aarav sent him crashing to the floor.

Gasps. Screams.

And then......

Taarika grabbed Aarav's hand.

"Let's go."

And just like that......

They ran.

......

The Escape

The moment they made it to the car, Aarav gunned the engine, tearing down the road.

Taarika's hands shook. Her heart raced.

Then, she turned to him.

And laughed.

Because they did it.

She was free.

Aarav glanced at her, his smirk victorious. "So... should we just get married now and piss them off even more?"

Taarika's breath caught.

Then.....

She grinned.

"Drive faster, Rockstar. We have a wedding to crash."

37
A Wedding Written in the Stars

Taarika's heart raced as the city lights blurred past the car window.

Aarav's hands were tight on the steering wheel, his jaw clenched. The adrenaline from their escape still buzzed in the air.

They had done it.

They had run away.

But now what?

Taarika turned to him, breathless. "Are we seriously doing this?"

Aarav glanced at her, eyes burning with determination. "I wasn't joking, Writer Girl. Let's get married."

Taarika's chest tightened.

She had always imagined her wedding differently—with family, traditions, a slow and careful decision.

But none of that mattered now.

All that mattered was him.

Aarav reached for her hand. "Say yes, Taarika."

Her fingers trembled in his.

Then......

She nodded.

Aarav grinned.

"Hold on tight. We have a wedding to crash."

....

The Temple of Fate

Aarav drove fast, weaving through the streets of Mumbai, searching for a temple.

They needed a place to get married. Now.

Finally.......

Through the misty glow of streetlights, they saw it.

A small, old temple, perched on a hill, the bells echoing in the night.

It felt like fate.

Taarika stepped out of the car, the night breeze cold against her skin, but Aarav's warmth beside her kept her steady.

He squeezed her hand. "Ready?"

She let out a breath. "With you? Always."

They ran up the steps, hearts pounding.

The temple priest looked startled as they approached. "Beta, this is an unusual time for a wedding."

Aarav grinned, out of breath. "Love doesn't check the time, Pandit ji."

The priest chuckled. "You have no family here?"

Taarika hesitated.

Aarav's smile faded. "They didn't give us a choice."

The priest sighed, studying them.

Then....he nodded. "Love is a bond beyond permission. Let's begin."

Taarika's heart swelled.

This was it.

No grand mandap. No crowd. No family blessings.

Just them.

Just love.

....

The Vows That Weren't Written

They stood before the fire, the sacred flames glowing between them.

Aarav held out his hand. "One last chance to run, Writer Girl."

Taarika smirked. "Shut up and marry me."

His grin was everything.

They took the seven sacred steps, each vow spoken from the depths of their hearts.

Step One: To share a life built on love.

Step Two: To support each other's dreams.

Step Three: To stand together, even when the world is against them.

Step Four: To never let fear decide their fate.

Step Five: To create a home in each other's arms.

Step Six: To grow old together, with laughter and music.

Step Seven: To choose each other.....every single day.

Taarika's eyes burned with tears, her hands shaking in his.

Aarav wiped a tear from her cheek, whispering, "I got you."

Her voice broke. "I know."

The priest blessed them, tying their hands together with sacred thread.

Husband. Wife.

Aarav pulled her close. "You're mine now."

Taarika laughed softly. "And you're mine."

He grinned. "So... can I kiss my wife now?"

She blushed. "You better."

And then.......

Under the temple bells, beneath the open sky, in the presence of only the gods and the stars.....

Aarav kissed his bride.

And the world finally made sense.

....

But Love Is Never That Easy...

They drove home in silence, the weight of what they had done settling in.

Aarav glanced at her. "Are you okay?"

Taarika exhaled. "We just got married."

Aarav smirked. "I know. Pretty hot, right?"

She laughed, but her heart was heavy.

Because her family...

They wouldn't accept this.

Would they ever forgive her?

Would they ever see that this wasn't a mistake?

And then......

Her phone buzzed.

She hesitated.

Aarav reached for her hand. "Whatever happens, we face it together."

Taarika swallowed hard.

And then.......

She picked up.

"Maa...?"

Silence.

Then—her mother's voice, cold and distant.

"You are no longer our daughter."

Taarika's breath caught.

Aarav stiffened beside her.

Her heart shattered.

And just like that..........

Their perfect night turned into their biggest battle yet.

38

Love Isn't a War, But I'll Fight for It

Taarika's voice broke.

"Maa… Papa…" Her breath trembled. "I'm still your daughter. Nothing has changed."

Her mother's gaze hardened. "Everything has changed."

Her father exhaled sharply, his voice cold. "You left us for a boy who knows nothing about family. You think love is enough? Love doesn't last. Family does."

Taarika flinched.

Her throat burned. "Then why can't I have both?"

Her father's silence was deafening.

She swallowed hard. "I didn't come here to fight. I came here to tell you that I love him. And I love you. And I will spend every single day proving to you that you haven't lost me."

Her mother's eyes glistened with something unreadable, but she didn't respond.

Her father turned away. "Go home, Taarika."

Taarika's chest ached.

Home.

The irony wasn't lost on her.

She was already home.....with Aarav.

And yet, her parents still held pieces of her heart she couldn't bear to lose.

But if they thought she was going to disappear, they were wrong.

Because she wasn't giving up.

....

Meanwhile, Aarav Had a Plan

When Taarika returned home, Aarav was waiting.

One look at her face, and he knew.

"They shut you out," he said softly.

She nodded, fighting the tears. "They think I betrayed them."

Aarav exhaled, running a hand through his hair.

Then.....

He smirked.

Taarika frowned. "Why do you look like you're planning something ridiculous?"

Aarav crossed his arms. "Because I am."

She groaned. "Aarav"

He took her hands, his voice serious now. "Taarika, I love you. But I know how much your family means to you. So if they won't come to us..."

Taarika blinked.

Aarav grinned.

"...Then I'll make them fall in love with me instead."

Her jaw dropped. "Wait...what?"

Aarav winked. "Watch me, Writer Girl."

....

Step One: Winning Over the Family, One Gesture at a Time

Aarav didn't barge into her house. He didn't argue.

Instead, he did what he did best—he spoke through actions.

First Gesture: Helping Without Asking

A week later, her father's car broke down outside the market.

He was stranded, frustrated, cursing under his breath.

And then.....

A bike pulled up beside him.

A familiar voice.

"Need a hand, Uncle?"

Her father turned, stunned.

Aarav, dressed in jeans and a black t-shirt, crouched down and examined the car engine, as if this was just another normal day.

Her father stared. "What are you doing here?"

Aarav smirked. "Saving you from cursing at an innocent vehicle."

Her father huffed. "I don't need your help."

Aarav raised a brow. "Really? Because it looks like your car is dead and you're stuck in 40-degree heat."

Silence.

Then...begrudgingly.....her father stepped aside.

Aarav grinned. "That's what I thought."

And without another word, he fixed the car.

Her father muttered something under his breath before saying, "You should've been a mechanic instead of a musician."

Aarav chuckled. "I'll take that as a compliment."

Her father didn't admit it, but later that evening, Taarika heard him mumble to her mother, "At least the boy knows something useful."

She smiled.

....

Second Gesture: Winning Over Her Mother's Heart Through Food

Two days later, her mother went to the temple in the morning, as she always did.

But when she returned home......

She found a basket of fresh vegetables, a handwritten note, and a thermos of homemade chai on the doorstep.

Her mother frowned, opening the note.

*"Aunty, I know you still hate me, but I remember how much you love morning chai. Hope this one makes your day better. - Aarav" *

Her mother's lips parted slightly.

She glanced around, but there was no sign of him.

She picked up the thermos, hesitated... then took a sip.

And for the first time in weeks, she didn't look angry.

....

Step Two: Getting an Invitation He Didn't Expect

A month passed.

Aarav kept showing up not at their house, but in their world.

Helping. Listening. Fixing small things they didn't ask for.

He never pushed. Never begged.

Just proved.

And then........

One evening, it happened.

Aarav was helping an old shopkeeper fix a sign outside the market when his phone buzzed.

Unknown Number: Dinner. 8 PM. Don't be late.

Aarav blinked.

Then grinned.

Because it was from Taarika's mother.

....

The Dinner That Changed Everything

Aarav showed up in a simple kurta, carrying a box of sweets.

Taarika met him at the door, wide-eyed.

"They actually invited you?" she whispered.

Aarav smirked. "What can I say? I'm irresistible."

She rolled her eyes, but her heart swelled.

Inside, the atmosphere was tense.

Her father barely looked at him. Her mother was neutral.

But Aarav?

Aarav was Aarav.

He cracked jokes. Helped serve the food. Complimented her mother's cooking so effortlessly that she almost smiled.

And then—the moment of truth.

Her father set down his spoon, looking directly at Aarav.

"You want my daughter's acceptance," he said slowly.

Aarav met his gaze. "No, Uncle. I want your acceptance."

A beat of silence.

Then.....

Her father leaned back. "Prove to me you can take care of her."

Aarav's eyes hardened with determination. "Tell me how."

Her father crossed his arms. "If you can do one thing....just one thing...that convinces me she'll never regret marrying you, I'll accept this marriage."

Taarika held her breath.

Aarav smiled. "Challenge accepted."

And just like that.....

The final test began.

39
The Final Test of Love

Aarav sat across from Taarika's father, eyes steady, hands firm on the table.

Her mother watched with cautious curiosity. Her uncle leaned back, observing like a judge at a trial.

And Taarika?

She was holding her breath, heart pounding in her chest.

Her father's voice was calm but sharp.

"You want my daughter? Then prove that you can handle responsibility."

Aarav didn't flinch. "How?"

Her father exhaled, crossing his arms. "You live in dreams, Aarav. Songs. Music. But life isn't a stage. A man needs to provide, to lead, to keep his family strong."

Aarav nodded slowly, understanding the weight of his words.

"Fine," Aarav said. "What do you want me to do?"

Her father leaned forward.

"If you can double the earnings of your café in three months, without any of Taarika's help, I'll accept you."

Gasps filled the room.

Taarika's jaw dropped. "Papa"

Her father raised a hand, silencing her.

Aarav smirked. "That's it?"

Her father narrowed his eyes. "You think it's easy?"

Aarav leaned back, confidence radiating from him. "No. But I think you just gave me the perfect challenge."

Her father studied him for a long moment. Then, he nodded.

The game was on.

....

The Café Challenge: Aarav vs. Time

For the next three months, Aarav became unstoppable.

Every morning, he was up before sunrise, studying business strategies, marketing plans, and financial reports.

Instead of just playing music, he started learning how to run a business.

He expanded the menu, collaborated with local influencers, and even launched a late-night acoustic series at the café.

And when the numbers started growing, he didn't stop.

Taarika watched in awe.

Because this wasn't just about winning her father's approval.

This was Aarav proving he was capable of more than just love songs and dreams.

This was him proving he could build a future for them.

....

The Final Day: The Results Are In

Three months later, they all gathered in the living room again.

Taarika's father sat at the head of the table, a spreadsheet in front of him.

The whole family leaned in as he checked the numbers.

Tension thickened the air.

Then....

A long pause.

Her father exhaled. Set the paper down.

And then, he did something no one expected.

He smiled.

A real, proud smile.

Aarav's lips twitched. "So?"

Her father nodded, his voice quiet but certain.

"You did it."

Taarika's heart exploded.

Aarav let out a breath and leaned back with a satisfied grin.

Her father looked at Aarav, something new in his eyes. "You proved me wrong, boy."

Aarav chuckled. "I get that a lot."

The room filled with laughter.

And then, her father stood up.

Aarav followed.

And just like that........

Her father extended his hand.

Aarav's grin softened. He took it firmly.

And in that single handshake, everything changed.

"You take care of my daughter," her father said gruffly.

Aarav's voice was steady.

"Always."

Taarika couldn't breathe.

She turned to her mother, who was watching with soft eyes.

Her mother stepped forward and, to everyone's shock, pulled Aarav into a hug.

"You're a fool," she murmured. "But a fool with a good heart."

Aarav chuckled. "I'll take it."

Taarika wiped her tears, unable to believe it.

It was happening.

Her family had accepted him.

Accepted them.

And suddenly.......

She was home again.

....

The Wedding Blessing That Meant Everything

A week later, in the same temple where they had married alone, they stood once more.

But this time........

Their families stood with them.

Taarika's mother placed a loving hand on her cheek. "You look beautiful, beta."

Taarika's heart swelled.

Her father nodded at Aarav, not with resistance, but with trust.

And as they took their vows again.....

With their families cheering instead of opposing.....

Taarika knew.

They had won.

Love had won.

And this?

This was only the beginning.

40

Love, Fame, and a Journey to Forever

The warm glow of fairy lights illuminated Chapters & Chords as laughter filled the air. The café had never been livelier.

Aarav and Taarika sat at their favorite corner, watching as their families—now united....finalized the details of something huge.

Their honeymoon.

Meera Kapoor, Aarav's mother, clapped her hands excitedly. "A trip to the Maldives! The perfect start to your married life."

Taarika's mother smiled warmly. "A beautiful place for a beautiful couple."

Taarika, still recovering from the whirlwind of her wedding blessings, blinked. "Wait, we're going where?"

Her father smirked. "It's all arranged. Flights, resort, everything."

Aarav grinned. "So, we're just being packed and shipped off like luggage?"

His mother rolled her eyes. "Don't be dramatic. It's a gift from all of us. Go, enjoy, and" she wiggled her brows, "make memories."

Taarika's face turned red. "Maa!"

Aarav smirked, throwing an arm around her. "I like where this is going."

Taarika groaned, but inside, her heart swelled.

A honeymoon. A fresh start. Just them.

What could be more perfect?

....

A Viral Surprise Before the Trip

Just when things couldn't get better, something unexpected happened.

A group of famous vloggers walked into Chapters & Chords the next afternoon.

Taarika had been behind the counter, adjusting the new menu, when she heard excited whispers among customers.

She looked up.....and froze.

Aarav, standing near the stage, raised an eyebrow. "Uh... why is everyone acting like we just got invaded by celebrities?"

Riya, who had been managing the social media, rushed toward them, eyes wide.

"Oh. My. God." She practically screamed. "Do you know who just walked in?!"

Taarika and Aarav exchanged glances. "Who?"

Riya grabbed her phone, showing them a YouTube channel with millions of subscribers.

"The Travel Chronicles...Exploring India's Hidden Gems."

Taarika's jaw dropped. "Wait. Are you saying....."

"Yes!" Riya bounced excitedly. "They're here to vlog about Chapters & Chords! It's going to be HUGE."

Aarav chuckled. "No pressure."

Taarika stared as the vloggers set up their cameras, talking animatedly about the cozy atmosphere, the music, and the unique concept of their writer's café + live music stage.

The lead vlogger, a young woman named Anaya, turned to the camera.

"This place is pure magic. A café where musicians and writers come together? Genius. And the love story behind it? Even better. Let's meet the couple who made it happen!"

Taarika's stomach flipped.

Anaya grinned. "Aarav and Taarika, can you join us for a little interview?"

Aarav smirked at Taarika. "Looks like we're famous, Mrs. Kapoor."

She rolled her eyes but smiled. "Fine. Let's do this."

....

The Interview That Changed Everything

The vloggers sat with them, recording every moment.

"So tell us," Anaya said, "Chapters & Chords is already a local favorite, but what inspired it?"

Taarika smiled, glancing at Aarav. "It started with a boy, a girl, and a dream."

Aarav smirked. "And a lot of coffee."

The audience laughed.

Taarika continued, "I've always believed that stories and music belong together. Aarav believed that music needs a place to breathe. So... we made this."

Anaya leaned in. "And your love story? The internet still talks about Aarav's viral proposal. Was it really a surprise?"

Taarika groaned, covering her face. "Oh, it was a shock."

Aarav chuckled. "Best risk I ever took."

Anaya turned to the camera.

"So here's the verdict, guys—this place isn't just a café. It's a home for dreamers. And something tells me that this is just the beginning for them."

The vlog ended with cheers and applause.

Within hours......

The video was trending.

Chapters & Chords was viral.

And Taarika and Aarav?

They had no idea what kind of homecoming was waiting for them after their honeymoon.

......

41

The Maldives: Love, Laughter, and Moonlit Waves

The moment they stepped off the plane, everything melted away.

No stress. No family drama. No expectations.

Just Aarav and Taarika.

Their resort was breathtaking—overwater villas, private beaches, candlelit dinners by the ocean.

Aarav, in sunglasses and a loose white shirt, stretched lazily. "This? This I could get used to."

Taarika, in a floral dress, smirked. "I'm surprised you're not carrying a guitar."

Aarav grinned. "Who says I didn't?"

She laughed, grabbing his hand.

The next few days were pure bliss....snorkelling in crystal-clear water, lazy afternoons in hammocks and moonlit dances on the sand.

One night, as they lay beneath the stars, Aarav turned to her.

"This is it, isn't it?"

Taarika blinked. "What?"

Aarav smiled. "Happiness."

She felt her heart squeeze.

Because he was right.

This was everything.

And she wouldn't trade it for the world.

....

A Surprise Homecoming

When they landed back in Mumbai, exhausted but glowing, they expected a quiet return.

Instead...........

They were greeted with cheers, music, and celebration.

The moment they stepped out of the car, Chapters & Chords was packed with customers, cameras, and reporters.

Taarika's eyes widened. "What is going on?"

Riya ran to them, grinning. "Oh, just the fact that you two are now officially the most talked-about café owners in the country."

Aarav raised a brow. "Come again?"

Riya waved her phone.

The Travel Chronicles video had crossed 10 million views.

Taarika's breath hitched. "Oh my god."

People held up signs.....

"Chapters & Chords: More Than a Café, It's a Love Story."

"The Couple Who Brought Music & Stories Together."

Aarav chuckled, pulling Taarika close. "Looks like we're famous, Writer Girl."

Taarika laughed, shaking her head. "We were just supposed to run a café, not take over the internet!"

Aarav winked. "Hey, when you marry a rockstar, things get wild."

She rolled her eyes but smiled.

They stepped inside their café...their dream, their home, their forever.

And as they watched their customers laughing, singing, and reading...

They knew.

This wasn't just a business.

This was their legacy.

And this?

This was just the beginning.

42
When the Music Fades

Taarika had always believed in stories with happy endings.

But nothing had prepared her for this.

Aarav was sick. And not the kind of sickness that a few days of rest and medicine could fix. This was something deeper—something that stole his energy, his music, his very essence.

It started subtly.

At first, it was just exhaustion. Long recording sessions drained him, but he brushed it off, saying it was the price of success. Then came the fevers—mild at first, then burning so fiercely that he had to cancel shows. His hands, the same hands that once danced over his guitar strings with effortless grace, started trembling.

By the time he collapsed on stage during a performance in Mumbai, there was no denying it anymore. Something was terribly wrong.

......

A Diagnosis That Changed Everything

The hospital room smelled of antiseptic and sterile walls. Aarav lay on the bed, eyes closed, his breathing shallow. Taarika sat beside him, gripping his hand tightly as if that alone could anchor him to her.

The doctor's words still rang in her ears.

"His immune system is severely compromised. It could be an autoimmune condition or something more serious. We need further tests."

Taarika had heard those words before. They were words that meant uncertainty. Words that meant waiting. Words that turned hope into fear.

When Aarav finally opened his eyes, his lips curved into a weak smile. "Hey, Writer Girl."

Taarika bit her lip to keep the tears at bay. "Hey, Musician."

He squeezed her fingers lightly. "Don't look at me like that. I'm not dying."

She let out a shaky breath. "Don't joke about that."

Aarav sighed, his gaze softening. "I'm sorry."

Silence stretched between them, thick with unspoken fears.

Then, in the quietest voice, he whispered, "I don't want to lose my music, Taarika."

And that was when she broke.

Because this wasn't just about him being sick. This was about the very thing that defined him slipping away.

....

A Love Stronger Than Fear

Taarika stayed with him through every test, every sleepless night, every moment of uncertainty.

She read to him when he was too tired to pick up a book. She played recordings of his own music when he was too weak to hold his guitar. She ran her fingers through his hair when the pain was too much to bear.

And one night, when he was at his lowest, when the weight of it all pressed down on him like an unbearable burden, she lay beside him and whispered, "Even if you can't play anymore, you'll always be music to me."

Aarav turned his face to her, eyes glistening. "You mean that?"

"With everything I am."

A single tear slipped down his cheek. "Then I think... I can fight this."

Taarika held him tighter. "We can fight this. Together."

....

When Fate Gives You a Choice

Days turned into weeks. The diagnosis came: a rare neurological condition affecting his motor skills. Not fatal, but progressive. Some days, he could play. Others, his fingers refused to move the way they used to.

The doctors suggested treatment, physical therapy, maybe even surgery. There were options. There was hope.

But there was also a choice to be made.

Stay in Mumbai, fight through the treatments, and cling to the dream he had worked so hard for?

Or return to Manesar, to a slower life, to the one person who had always seen him beyond the music?

One evening, as they sat on the rooftop, Aarav turned to Taarika. "If I can't play like I used to... do you think people will still listen?"

Taarika smiled, taking his hand in hers. "Your music isn't in your fingers, Aarav. It's in you. And the people who truly love your songs? They'll hear you, no matter what."

Aarav exhaled, closing his eyes for a long moment. Then, when he opened them, there was something steady in his gaze.

"Let's go home."

Taarika's heart swelled. "Home?"

Aarav nodded. "Manesar. Let's build Chapters & Chords together. Let's write a different kind of song."

Taarika blinked back tears. "You're sure?"

He smiled, pressing a soft kiss to her forehead. "The only thing I've ever been sure about... is you."

....

A New Beginning

They left Mumbai a week later.

Not as an ending, but as a new chapter.

Aarav's music didn't stop. It changed. He learned to compose, to teach, to find melodies in places he never had before. And Taarika? She wrote their story, one page at a time, in the heart of the café they built together.

Because love wasn't about holding on to the past.

It was about creating a future.

And as Aarav played a soft tune on the piano one evening—his fingers moving slower, but his heart still full—Taarika sat beside him, knowing that no matter what happened next, they had already found their forever.

Together.

43

Love in Every Heartbeat

The warm glow of Manesar's evening sky bathed Chapters & Chords in golden hues, the scent of freshly brewed coffee and old books filling the café. Aarav sat by the grand window, his fingers gently moving over the piano keys, playing a melody that had no name yet—but it was soft, full of hope, like the quiet promise of a new beginning.

Taarika watched him from behind the counter, her heart swelling with love. Months had passed since they returned from Mumbai, and life had settled into something beautiful. Aarav's hands weren't as quick as they once were, but his music hadn't faded—it had simply transformed.

And so had they.

Taarika placed a hand over her stomach, a secret smile playing on her lips. She had been waiting for the right moment. Waiting for the perfect way to tell him. And now, as she watched him hum softly, lost in the music, she knew—this was it.

....

A Surprise Written Between the Lines

That evening, after closing the café, Taarika led Aarav to their favorite spot—the rooftop where they had shared so many memories. The lanterns were lit, the stars scattered above them like tiny fireflies, and the cool breeze carried the distant hum of the town.

Aarav stretched, letting out a content sigh. "You've been smiling all day," he teased, wrapping an arm around her. "What's going on in that brilliant writer mind of yours?"

Taarika bit her lip, excitement bubbling inside her. "I, um... I have something for you."

Aarav raised an eyebrow. "Oh? A new poem? A song?"

She shook her head, handing him a small notebook. "Just read it."

Curious, Aarav flipped open the first page. His eyes scanned the words, his expression shifting from confusion to realization.

"Our story began with music, with words written between the lines. But now, a new chapter is beginning... a chapter written with tiny heartbeats, with lullabies waiting to be sung. A chapter where 'we' becomes 'three.'"

Aarav's breath hitched. He reread the words, as if making sure he wasn't imagining them. Slowly, he looked up at her, his voice barely above a whisper.

"Taarika... are you...?"

She nodded, eyes shimmering with unshed tears. "Yes."

Aarav exhaled sharply, running a hand through his hair as laughter bubbled out of him—pure, disbelieving joy. "You're pregnant?"

She let out a soft giggle. "We're pregnant."

Before she could say another word, he pulled her into his arms, lifting her off the ground as he spun her around. She squealed, laughing as he buried his face in her neck.

"I love you," he murmured against her skin. "I love you so much."

Taarika clung to him, her heart racing. "I love you more, Musician."

They stayed like that, wrapped in each other's arms, until the stars above blurred into nothing but a sea of light.

But the surprises weren't over yet.

....

A Doctor's Unexpected News

A week later, Aarav insisted on accompanying Taarika for her first ultrasound. He held her hand tightly as they sat in the doctor's office, nervous but excited.

The doctor smiled as she applied the cool gel to Taarika's stomach. "Let's take a look, shall we?"

Aarav squeezed Taarika's hand, his eyes locked onto the screen. The sound of a heartbeat filled the room.....fast, steady, beautiful.

But then...

Another heartbeat.

Taarika's eyes widened. Aarav's grip on her hand tightened.

The doctor chuckled at their stunned faces. "Well, I was going to break it to you gently, but—congratulations! You're having twins."

Silence.

Pure, stunned silence.

Taarika's mouth fell open. "Twins?" she whispered, as if saying it louder would make it more real.

Aarav blinked. Then again. Then, suddenly.........

He burst out laughing.

Taarika turned to him in shock. "Aarav?"

He shook his head, still grinning. "Of course. Of course, we're having twins! You're the love of my life, my muse, my greatest plot twist....why would our love story be anything less than extraordinary?"

Taarika let out a breathless laugh, wiping away the happy tears that escaped. "We're going to be parents to two babies, Aarav."

Aarav leaned down, pressing a kiss to her forehead before placing a hand over her stomach. "Hey, little ones," he murmured. "I'm your dad. And I promise, no matter what happens, you will always be loved."

Taarika watched him with wonder, her heart aching with happiness.

This...this was the man she had fallen in love with. A man who found music in everything, even in life's unexpected surprises.

And as they left the doctor's office, hand in hand, their hearts lighter than ever, one thing was certain.....

Their greatest song was just beginning

44
The Song Between the Pages

The evening sky over Manesar was painted in shades of lavender and gold, as the soft hum of music intertwined with the scent of freshly brewed coffee and old books. Inside Chapters & Chords, the café that Aarav and Taarika had built with love and dreams, laughter and warmth filled the air.

This place wasn't just a café. It was a story....a living, breathing testament to love, music, and words.

Aarav stood on the small stage in the corner, his guitar resting on his lap. Taarika sat beside him, a book open in her hands, her fingers tracing the words she had once only dreamed of publishing. And between them, giggling and arguing in their own little world, were their twins.....Rehan and Saanvi.

Rehan, named after the Arabic word for 'fragrance,' symbolizing the lingering beauty of music, held a toy guitar, mimicking his father's every move. Saanvi, whose name meant 'knowledge' and 'writing,' clutched a tiny notebook and a pink pen, scribbling down what she called "the greatest story ever told."

Aarav watched them with a soft smile, his heart swelling. "Who told you it was the greatest story?"

Saanvi pouted, tapping the pen against her chin. "Mommy says every story is the greatest if it's written with love."

Taarika glanced up from her book, raising an eyebrow. "And she's right."

Rehan strummed his little guitar, tilting his head. "And what about songs, Daddy? Are they the greatest if they're played with love?"

Aarav's fingers gently moved over his guitar strings, playing the first few notes of an old melody....a melody that had once been unfinished, lingering in his heart, waiting for words.

"A song is just a story with a heartbeat," he said softly.

Taarika smiled at him, that same knowing smile she had given him all those years ago in Caffeine & Chapters when their journey had begun.

As if on cue, Rehan and Saanvi squealed in excitement. "Play the song, Daddy! The one you wrote for Mommy!"

Aarav chuckled, glancing at Taarika, who simply shook her head, amused.

"Do I have a choice?" he asked.

"Not when it's about me," she teased, nudging him with her shoulder.

With that, Aarav began to strum, his voice carrying through the café, as familiar as the love that had weathered every storm, as strong as the dreams they had never given up on.

**"The world wrote our story in spaces unseen,

Between the music, between the words,

And every chord played, every page turned,

Led me right back to you."**

Taarika closed her eyes, letting the melody wash over her, feeling every memory, every heartbreak, every choice that had led them here.

This was their song. This was their story.

She looked at the young faces in the audience, eyes wide with admiration, hearts full of dreams.

There was a time when she and Aarav had been like them...two souls chasing the impossible, torn between love and ambition, afraid of choosing one over the other.

And now, sitting here, wrapped in love, in music, in words, she knew the truth.

You don't have to choose between love and dreams. You can have both. You just have to fight for them.

She set down her book, turning to the crowd.

"You know," she said, her voice steady but warm, "for the longest time, Aarav and I thought our dreams had to be separate. That love was a distraction, or that choosing love meant letting go of ambition."

Aarav nodded, strumming his guitar lightly. "But we were wrong."

Taarika smiled. "Because love isn't about sacrificing your dreams. It's about having someone who believes in them as much as you do."

A young girl in the front row raised her hand hesitantly. "But what if dreams take you in different directions?"

Aarav exchanged a glance with Taarika before setting his guitar down.

"Dreams might take you down different roads," he said gently, "but if the love is real, you'll always find your way back to each other."

The café was silent, the weight of his words settling in.

Taarika reached for his hand, squeezing it. "And sometimes, if you're really lucky, your dreams and love can become the same thing."

She gestured around them...at the café, at the books, at the stage, at the two little souls who were a blend of music and words, of love and destiny.

"This is ours," she whispered. "This is Chapters & Chords. Our story, our song, our forever."

Tears shimmered in the eyes of a few in the audience, but they were happy tears....the kind that made hearts lighter, the kind that made souls believe in possibilities.

Because that's what Chapters & Chords was.

A place where words met melodies.

A place where love and dreams didn't have to be separate.

A place where every story, every song, every heart found a home.

And as Aarav strummed the final note and Taarika turned the last page, they knew........

Some stories don't end.

Some songs never fade.

Because love, when real, is infinite.

And so, they played on.

Forever.

....

The End... and The Beginning.

9 798899 060434